Turned Up

Hot Shot Series

Clifford "Spud" Johnson

www.urbanbooks.net

Urban Books, LLC
300 Farmingdale Road, N.Y.-Route 109
Farmingdale, NY 11735

Turned Up: Hot Shot Series

ISBN 13: 978-1-64556-348-8
ISBN 10: 1-64556-348-0

First Trade Paperback Printing May 2023
Printed in the United States of America

10 9 8 7 6 5 4 3 2 1

Distributed by Kensington Publishing Corp.
Submit Orders to:
Customer Service
400 Hahn Road
Westminster, MD 21157-4627
Phone: 1-800-733-3000
Fax: 1-800-659-2436

When I get to the point that I don't care about my life, beware . . . because I *definitely* won't care about yours.

—*Hot Shot*

Dedication

I'd like to dedicate my seventeenth book to my two closest relatives, James R. Brown II (Jay) and Hakeem B. Carr (Bill). May they continue to rest peacefully.

Prologue

Hot Shot couldn't believe that the director of the FBI had pulled some strings to have Nola released. He was standing outside the federal camp when he watched his heartbeat, his wife, Nola Gaines, the woman he loved more than anything in the world.

She exited the federal prison camp and stepped toward him with a grin on her face. "So, you got it like that, huh? You made this happen and didn't tell me, Shot?"

"You're supposed to be in my arms right now, giving me a tight hug, but no, you wanna start fussing at me out the gate. This married stuff may be too much for a man of my stature to handle." They both laughed and embraced tightly, sharing a long and passionate kiss. Hot Shot was the first to break their embrace, smiled, and said, "Now, *that's* the proper way to greet your husband. I expect that daily." He easily ducked the punch she threw at him, grabbed her bag with one hand and her hand with the other, and led her to the rental car parked in the parking lot of the federal prison. Once they were inside the car and on their way, Hot Shot began to explain how things would be.

"So, we're living in L.A.? When can I tell my sister I'm out, Shot?"

"That's going to be kinda hard to do, baby. I need to get at JT and see how he wants to handle that situation. I in no way want to keep you away from your sister, but it's crucial that what I do remains a secret. Cotton doesn't even know."

"I understand, baby, but it's only going to be a matter of time before Lola figures out that something ain't right. Like when I don't call her for our every-other-week phone call, especially when it comes to our once-a-month visit. So I think you should make sure JT covers *that* base because Lola will blow up the spot once she isn't able to speak to me."

Hot Shot nodded his head in agreement and said, "Facts. I'll get at JT and let him know the severity of the situation."

"While you do that, you might as well tell him to let you get at Cotton because, sooner or later, that too can blow up the spot. That man has the utmost respect for you. Hell, he'd love to be able to assist you any way he can."

As Hot Shot pulled the car into the rental return slot, they got out of the vehicle and held hands as he led Nola toward the private airstrip where a shiny GV was waiting for them. They entered the plane, were greeted by the pilot, and quickly went to their seats.

"You like?"

"You do know we are way past the impress-me stage, Shot. I've loved you since I first saw you at that club. I'm so in love with you, sir, that my heart beats faster when I'm near you," she said as she grabbed his hand and placed it over her heart. Her heart was beating so fast he thought she would have a heart attack.

She smiled at the look on her husband's face and said, "See, I told you. But to answer your question, yes, I like, but you know what I would like even better than this pretty plane?"

"What?"

"I've never had sex on a plane before, especially in a private jet. I need to feel you inside of me—*now*."

The urgency in her voice gave him the hardest hard-on he'd ever had in his life. He quickly unbuckled his belt, pulled his pants down, and watched Nola as she slid off her jeans, dropped to her knees, and put her hot mouth around his swollen dick. Hot Shot felt as if he was going to explode inside her mouth. She sucked him slowly at first. Then she sped up, and Hot Shot could no longer hold back.

"Nola," he hissed, "I'm coming." She went even faster and caught every drop of his cum inside her mouth.

"Now, *that* was a nice surprise. I needed that."

Shot sat down in his seat and tried to catch his breath. Once he was breathing normally, he smiled at her and said, "You freak."

"You love it."

He smiled and said, "Yes, baby, I do."

"Before we get to the real business, what does JT have in store for your next move? I hope he knows I plan on going with you when you go to work."

Laughing, he said, "I'm not sure about that, but we won't have to worry about any of that right now because I'm working on my home turf."

She stared at him for a few seconds, then said, "You working in Cali on what, Shot?"

He returned her stare and said, "Yes, working on guns from the Inglewood 13 Mexican gang."

"I remember the stuff you told me when you visited me. Are you sure you'll be able to focus on your assignment without letting your personal situation affect your judgment?"

"I'm a professional. I take pride in my work, but I will keep it all the way real. This assignment is personal. I want—no—I *intend* on bringing pain to those Mexicans. My job is to bring down the key factors in the gang. I *will* find out who killed my family. I now know *why* it happened, so that makes me feel a tad bit better. Now, it's time to find out who did it and who made the call for it to be done. I'm going to murder them, baby. No jail—only death."

"So be it. I know how much the loss of your family hurts you. My job is to have your back at all times. Like you told me when you were in the marines, you guys always had one another's six. Well, you have me and Cotton watching your six."

"Right."

"So, we are about to get turned up in Inglewood."

"Yes, we're about to get turned up, baby."

"Cool. Now, let's get turned *all* the way up on this jet. Your wife needs to get broken off real good, mister."

He smiled and said, "No worries, baby. I can definitely turn up for *your* needs." And he was a man of his word as they were turned up sexually for the duration of their flight on the GV headed to sunny California.

Chapter One

Cotton's eyes opened wide in shock when he saw Hot Shot and Nola enter the house. He has been Hot Shot's right-hand man since they met in Dallas, Texas. He stood, and with two strides, he was in front of Nola with his arms open and gave her a tight hug.

"Welcome home, Nola. You're looking good as ever," he said as he released her from their embrace.

"Thank you, Cotton. I know you're loving it here in La La Land."

"Yeah, it's cool. The females are a trip, though. A man has to have paper to deal with these females on a daily basis. Every time I leave the house, I'm spending ends and not feeling that at all. But you know me. I'm a country boy that's going to make it do what it does. And best believe these L.A. women got their hands full dealing with me." He paused and stared at Hot Shot and Nola for a minute, then said, "Wait a minute. How you get out? I thought you still had a couple of more years to do."

"Cotton, I need to get at you about something serious, so let's sit down for a minute so we can put this together," Hot Shot said as he led them to the living room where they sat. Hot Shot really didn't like deceiving Cotton like he'd been doing. Over the last few years, Cotton had become like a brother to him. It was time to put everything on the table. If it cost him his friendship with Cotton, then so be it. He had a job to do, and nothing or no one would ever stop him. He took a deep breath and said,

"I'm a federal agent, Cotton. I've been working under-cover for the FBI."

Cotton smiled at Hot Shot and Nola and said, "Damn, why y'all looking all gloomy and shit? Boss man, I may be a country boy, but there's nothing green about me. I figured you were plugged into some heavy people. I didn't think it was the FBI, but I knew it was some form of law enforcement. How you move showed me that a long time ago."

"How I move?" Hot Shot asked curiously.

"Yeah, whenever JT calls or comes through, you act differently. It's like your body lingo switches up, like you talking to a superior like in the army or some shit. I can't really explain it. All I knew was you weren't making all the moves you make on some straight illegal shit—which is cool with me. As long I get this money and stay lit, I don't give a damn. I also knew that you'd tell me when you felt I needed to know. So, now that you know I know you're a superagent, does that change anything about us, Boss man?"

Shaking his head, Hot Shot stood, gave his main man a hug, and told him, "No, it doesn't change a thing. You my guy, and you will always be my guy." They gave each other another hug, and it was all good.

"OK, now we got that out of the way, can you show me to my room so I can take a hot bath and enjoy the rest of my first day home?" Nola said, and they all laughed.

While Nola was getting herself together, Hot Shot called JT and told him about the conversation he just had with Cotton. He also informed him how Nola felt about wanting to be able to talk to her sister.

In his usual Kentucky drawl, JT said, "Well, hell, you told everybody else. Why not tell her sister too? What harm can it do at this point?"

Hot Shot pondered his words for a moment and said, "I don't know. What if she told her that her brother and cousins were in federal prison because of me? How do I know she will not be all twisted and angry with me?"

"You're not giving her the high hard one, so who cares if she's mad at you? Either way, that's your call. Let's get to the matter at hand. That young amigo Toker will be giving you a call for a meeting. Then you can take it from there. Again, I know this is personal for you, too personal if you ask me, but I trust you to remain disciplined and get the job done. Any collateral damage . . . Hell, shit happens, but I want you to make sure that it ain't too much. Are we clear, Hot Shot?"

"Yep." Hot Shot ended the call, went into his bedroom, and sat down on the bed with a smile as he listened to his wife sing while soaking in the bathtub. He took off his clothes and went into the bathroom and joined her. Toker and the Inglewood 13s were the last things on his mind.

Cotton was lying on the couch, talking to one of the many new females he'd met since moving to Los Angeles. He was touching more money than he ever had in his life. There was no way he would mess up this arrangement with Hot Shot. He didn't give a damn if he was a federal agent. As long as he could keep getting that money, he was straight. He laughed aloud as he realized he had a fucking get-out-of-jail-free card. His life was smooth sailing now, and he was loving the ride.

"So, check this out, baby. What are you trying to do tonight? I'm trying to go get some good seafood, then go back to your place so I can eat that cat. If you're with that, I'll come scoop you in a couple of hours."

"That's cool. I'll drop a pin so you can come get me. Where are we going to eat, boo?" the female Cotton was talking to on the phone asked.

"Didn't you say you lived in Long Beach?"

"Yeah."

"OK, we'll grab something out at the Pike."

"That's cool. You know it may be cold out by the beach."

"No worries, baby. Cotton will keep you warm all night long."

"I'm sure you will," the young lady said as they ended their call.

"Money, pussy, and more money. Shit, I love L.A." Cotton got up and headed to his room, humming.

Chapter Two

Hot Shot was standing outside the Habit Grill burger restaurant waiting for Toker, the young Hispanic snitch that would help him bring down some heavyweights in the violent Mexican gang known as the Inglewood 13s. He remembered Toker from when his little brother used to hang out. He hoped he wouldn't have to hurt him. But if he did, he really didn't give a damn. He had murder on his mind and a pained soul. There would be a lot of blood spilled on these Inglewood streets, that's for damn sure, he vowed as he continued to survey his surroundings and wait for Toker.

As he was about to text him again, Toker pulled into the parking lot in a black Audi SUV. He motioned for Hot Shot to come into his vehicle. Then Toker eased the car into traffic on Century Boulevard. He made a left turn on Crenshaw Boulevard and continued in silence.

Slightly agitated by the silence, Hot Shot said, "What's good, Toker? How is this meeting going to go down?"

"I'm waiting for my homie to get at me, and then we're going to meet two other homies, Termite and his little brother Puma. They're the ones who are in charge of getting guns for us. You have to understand how hard it was for me to get this meeting. You've been gone a long time, Jason. Things have changed. We rarely deal with Blacks."

"When did this change? Inglewood 13s always got along with Inglewood Bloods. Wasn't your beef mainly with the Lennox 13s?"

"That beef will never stop. The thing is, now us South-siders all fall under Sureno. So we still have our beefs with each other, but we have beef with all Blacks in Inglewood."

"So you're telling me that the Mexicans are on some beef with everyone in Inglewood that's Black?"

"Yep. Times have changed, and the rules are different now, Jason."

"Stop calling me by my real name. I'm Hot Shot or Shot. I don't want your people to connect me to my brother. Speaking of my brother, how did that really go down, Toker?"

Toker sighed and said, "You know me and Jeremy been cool since we went to elementary school. He saw how I was on the come-up, and he wanted in. So, I would slide him a little something just to keep some money in his pockets. It was cool. Then he started to want more and more. He wasn't spending his money. All he wanted was more drugs so he could slang and keep stacking his bread. He got up to buying two kilos a month. It was all good until my people wanted to meet him. At that time, there wasn't any beef going on, so I set up the meeting and introduced Jeremy to my homie, Casper. After that, Jeremy stopped scoring from me and dealt only with Casper."

"So, this Casper guy is the man who did that to my family?"

"No. Maybe. I'm not sure. All I do know is me and Jeremy got jacked by the 18s, and it all went bad after that. Shit, there was a hit attempt on *my* life, but they missed. The only reason I was spared was that I have a cousin that's high enough in rank that got me a pass."

"You got a pass, and my family didn't. I want to know who killed my family, Toker. I want to know who gave the order to have my family killed. Do you understand me?"

"I hear you, Shot. Honestly, for a hit to be approved, it has to come from the top, and the top man is Franco. Period. There are several hitters from the neighborhood, but the ones I feel are ruthless enough to do what they did to your family are Paco and Devil. They are some cold fuckers, homes, for real. Like I said, I'm not sure, but in my gut, I feel they're the guys you want."

"And you're back in with your homies because of your cousin?"

"Right, homes."

"Since Casper was in charge of the drug parts of things, he's the one who put the hit out on you and my brother. That's what makes sense to me."

"Nah, Casper's scary ass ain't built like that. He acts hard, but he's soft. Franco gave the order. I'm damn sure about that."

"Okay. This Termite and Puma will do business with guns, but what about drugs?"

Toker laughed and said, "Nah, there will be no drug talk with those two. Plus, the drug connection is secure. You do that, and you will get them suspicious. Please, don't do that. I'm skating on thin ice as it is, so you cannot slip, or we're both dead."

"Understood."

Toker received a phone call and was told where the meeting would take place. He disconnected the call and told Hot Shot they were meeting Termite and Puma at Inglewood Cemetery. "Remember, homes, no slips. We know each other from around the way, and we bumped into each other a few weeks ago. No need to go into detail because they will watch your reactions to everything you say. Before the talk about weapons takes place, they'll try to feel you out. If they think they have tripped you up, then it's a wrap."

"No worries. I know what I'm doing. Once things move along and I start doing business, we will not need to communicate unless you have some pertinent information I need. Still, get at JT once I'm in. I'll take it from there."

"I feel you," Toker said as he drove his car through Inglewood Cemetery toward the destination he was to go to. When he saw his two homeboys, Termite and Puma, kneeling under a tree, he parked the SUV, got out, and told Hot Shot, "I gotta pat you down, so if you strapped, you're going to have to give it up."

"Are they holding?"

"Definitely."

"Then why do *I* have to give up *my* weapon?"

Toker rolled his light gray eyes and gave Hot Shot an exasperated look as he searched him. After he relieved Hot Shot of his 9 mm, he said, "This is the start. You handle your shit now, and you'll get to the end of this shit, hopefully, alive."

Toker stepped away from Hot Shot, nodded toward his homeboys, and mumbled a silent prayer: *Please, let this go right, Father.*

Hot Shot stepped onto the grass and over grave sites until he stood in front of the two Inglewood 13 gang members dressed in typical Los Angeles gang member garb: black Dickie pants and white tee shirts. As he was being closely scrutinized, he never let his gaze leave the two men in front of him, showing no signs of nervousness or fear. He may not have his weapon on him, but he was confident if something were to arise between himself and the two men in front of him, he would be able to defend himself adequately. His Special Forces training assured him of that. That's why before he spoke, he made sure that he was close enough to strike if need be.

"What's good, gentlemen?" asked Hot Shot.

Both men stared at him with frowns on their faces. Then the shorter of the two said something in Spanish to his homeboy. His homeboy didn't speak but nodded. Hot Shot felt it would be to his advantage not to let the two men know that he was fluent in Spanish. So he stood there and waited for them to speak, acting as if he didn't realize that the guy had told his brother that Hot Shot didn't look like too much of nothing.

"What up, homie? What you got for us? We don't have time for too much talk. Me and my li'l bro have a busy schedule, so talk," Termite said.

"It's not about what I got for you but more about what you need from *me*. I have a large range of weapons, so what do you guys want?" Hot Shot asked, never once losing eye contact with the gang members.

Nodding, Termite said, "We need some heavy shit. AR-15s, AK-47s mostly, and some pistols too, nines."

"You get more than a case of ARs, and I'll give them to you for two thousand apiece; same for the AKs. I can give you the nines for 800 apiece again if you get more than a case."

"How many come in a case?" asked Puma, finally joining the conversation.

"Twenty-five in each case of assault rifles. Fifty in each case of pistols."

The two men exchanged glances, then Puma said, "We can do better than those, homes. We'll move with you if you can get at us with $1,800 apiece on the assault weapons. As for the nines, we're not trying to spend more than $650 apiece."

Hot Shot shook his head and said, "I apologize for wasting your time, gentlemen, because I am not here to negotiate. I've given you my prices."

Termite and Puma shared a quick back-and-forth conversation in rapid Spanish. Termite told Puma that Hot Shot's prices were okay, whereas Puma said, "Let's just agree to his terms and jack this square-looking fool."

Hot Shot felt it was time to turn up on the situation, and in rapid Spanish of his own, he told the brothers,

"You should listen to your brother, Puma. My prices are good. And if you think you can take anything from me, that would be a major mistake. No man has ever, or will ever, take *anything* from me and live to talk about it. So, either we're going to do some business, or let's end this now."

Both men wore shocked expressions after hearing Hot Shot speak their native language. Termite smiled while Puma frowned in annoyance. "If we agree to your numbers, when can we make it happen?"

"What do you want to start with?"

"Two cases of everything," said Termite.

Hot Shot smiled as he made the mental calculations and answered, "That's $100,000 for fifty assault weapons and $40,000 for the nines. $140,000 total. I can have everything lined up for you by next Friday."

Puma was about to say something in Spanish to his brother but stopped and said, "What do you think, Termite?"

"Fuck it, homes. Let's see what this Hot Shot can do."

Hot Shot smiled and said, "We move how I say we move. When I'm ready to deliver the goods, you will have Toker bring me the money to where I say. Then I'll personally deliver the weapons. These are my terms, and they aren't up for debate, especially after hearing your brother speak on taking something from me. Do we have a deal, gentlemen?"

Termite scowled at his brother, but to Hot Shot, said, "Yeah, we got a deal, homes."

Hot Shot smiled, shook their hands, turned, and confidently strolled toward Toker's SUV. Once he was inside and Toker pulled away, Toker asked, "How did it go, Hot Shot?"

"Looks like the I-13s are in business with Hot Shot."

Chapter Three

After Toker dropped Hot Shot off back at his car, Hot Shot called JT and let him know how the meeting went and what the Mexican gang members wanted.

"So, I assume the meeting went smoothly, son?" asked JT.

"Of course. I need those weapons ASAP. After I make the deal, I think they will be comfortable moving forward. Toker told me how the Inglewood 13s and other Mexican gangs are at war with the Bloods and Crips in L.A. That fact alone tells me they will want more weapons."

"Good, really good, son. Now, were you able to learn anything about the family issue?" JT asked with concern in his voice. He was worried that Hot Shot's focus would be on finding out what happened to his family rather than the mission at hand. Operation Cleanup had started out better than anyone expected. But bringing Hot Shot to L.A. to deal with the Mexican gangs was pushing it a little too much as far as he was concerned. However, the director gave the orders, and he had to follow them. He prayed that Hot Shot didn't lose it.

"Toker explained some things to me that gave me the answer about why it was done to my family and who the Mexicans were who actually murdered them. I'm sure I'll learn more as time goes by."

"All right, son, I'll get everything in motion and have what you need before Friday. How's your wife enjoying her freedom?"

"She's loving it."

"Good, that's real good. The director felt you deserved that and hoped you would continue to do good on the mission."

"I appreciate what he has done for my wife. I won't fail. I will continue to do what I do. You just remember that it takes some bad to do some good. In this Inglewood 13s' mission, there will definitely be bad before the good, JT."

JT sighed and said, "Be careful, son," and ended the call.

Hot Shot was smiling as he pulled his car into the garage. When he entered the house, he saw Cotton sitting on the couch with his phone in his hand, laughing loudly. He nodded as he passed and went upstairs to his bedroom. Nola was napping in the bed, so he tried not to disturb her. Just as he was leaving the bedroom, she opened her eyes.

"What are you doing, Shot?"

"Trying not to disturb you, baby."

She sat up, smiled at her husband, and said, "Don't ever worry about disturbing me, baby. You can wake me up anytime you want. Now, come here and come play with this cat."

He watched his wife as she pulled the covers off her, exposing her beautiful, well toned body. He groaned and smiled at her as he started to remove his clothes. They made love, then fell asleep in each other's arms, totally content.

The next morning after enjoying a hearty breakfast, Hot Shot and Cotton took Nola shopping. Originally, Hot Shot wanted to give his wife the debit card and let her go and enjoy herself, with Cotton being her driver. But Nola wasn't having any of that. She wanted her husband to join them. So here he was, stuck holding bags as they walked through the Beverly Center. Hot Shot couldn't understand how a woman could be so meticulous. They went from store to store, spending a minimum of fifteen minutes in each. Then Nola became starstruck whenever she saw an actor, actress, rapper, or athlete. So that took up more time as she had to get a selfie. Finally, they headed to the car, and Nola informed them that she needed to get a manicure and a pedicure, but she wouldn't put them through that and gave them the go-ahead to drop her off at the nail shop she spotted by the house. Both Hot Shot and Cotton were relieved that this ordeal had finally come to an end.

"Damn, Nola, are you sure you don't need anything else? I mean, Rodeo Drive isn't that far from here. We could go spend another five hours shopping there if you like," Cotton said sarcastically.

Hot Shot laughed. The look Nola gave him quickly stopped his laughter.

"Just get me to the damn nail shop, and you two jokers can go do whatever y'all need to do."

"Your wish is my command, baby," Hot Shot said as he led the way out of the mall.

After dropping off Nola, Hot Shot told Cotton about the meeting he had with the I-13s and that he wanted him to accompany him for the transaction Friday.

"Damn, Boss man, they getting that much firepower? What they trying to do, start a fucking war?"

"Seems like it. According to Toker, the Mexican gangs are at war with the Black gangs."

"The Bloods and the Crips?"

"Yep."

"That's crazy. Those guys may need some heat too. Are you going to get at them to see?"

Shaking his head, Hot Shot said, "No. This mission is to get at the Mexicans. Unless I'm told differently, that's the way it remains."

"I feel you. I'm just feeling like, damn, we're strapping these Mexicans with all these weapons, putting our people out here at a big disadvantage."

"That's true, and as a Black man, I'm in total agreement with you. But as a federal agent, that's not my concern. That sounds cold, I know, but it is what it is. Look at it this way . . . We're about to take a lot of the I-13s off the streets, so that will help the Bloods and Crips in Inglewood greatly."

"Facts. So how are we going about dealing with them?"

"Each weapon they buy will have a GPS tracker inside of it. We'll wait a few days, maybe a week tops, then send in the boys to make arrests."

"If that's how it's going to go down, then there's no worry about them Mexicans putting in any work on the Bloods and Crips. Shit, they won't have any time unless they get right at them once they buy the guns."

"Right. My head is all over the place right now. What's most important to me at the moment is getting the I-13s that murdered my family. Toker gave me the information I needed. I just have to be patient until I can get more information so I can get them and bring the pain."

"I feel you, Boss man, and you know I'm with you all the way."

Hot Shot smiled at his right-hand man. "Thanks, Cotton, I appreciate that. I really hated keeping things from you. You're my bro, and I should have kept it real with you, but the job stopped me."

"I'm not tripping on any of that, Boss man. As long as I keep my get-outta-jail-free card, I'm good."

"You're something else. Come on. There's a few stops we need to make."

"How long will it take us? I got this freaky li'l thang I'm trying to touch up."

"How do you meet all these women?"

Cotton smiled, and his pearly white teeth were bright in contrast to his dark skin. "Facebook dating. I've met some bad females there. This female I'm trying to smash, Tameka, oh my God, Boss man, she has a body outta this world. Her walk is nasty. I mean, it just makes you want to snatch up her ass and get down right there."

"Where does she stay?"

"Off 107th and Vermont."

"Be careful where you go. Some places ain't safe for an out-of-towner. If my memory serves me right, 107th and Vermont is 107 Hoover Crips."

"Man, that gang bang shit don't bother me. I wish one of those fools would try to test my gangsta. I'll give it to them just how you showed me. All the hours at the gun range with you will give me the advantage over those drive-by shooters. Oh, and that was another clue you gave me to make me think you were more than you told me. That army training smoke you were sending me was funny. I'm good, though. You trained me solidly. So, what are we getting into?"

"Nothing really; just bending some corners, looking at some things. I want the meeting to be somewhere we'll have complete control of the situation. Once Toker brings you the money, I'll get with them. It's important that you have eyes on me at all times."

"Right. Where are we going to meet them?"

"We're about to bend some corners and see now. I wanna keep it on the north side of Inglewood, so they'll remain comfortable." Hot Shot snapped his fingers and said, "I got it."

Fifteen minutes later, Hot Shot parked his Audi in front of Hillcrest Continuation, a school for the kids that were not doing right in their local schools. Hot Shot and Cotton got out of the car, and Hot Shot began running down how he wanted things to go with the I-13s.

"I'll have Toker meet you there," Hot Shot pointed toward the football field around the corner from where they were. "After he leaves, you will be able to see me from Sentinel Field. I'll be here before them to ensure everything is kosher, but I want you to remain on point at all times. Don't take anything lightly. If you see something you even *think* could be a problem, let me know."

"I got you, Boss man. You say you got info on those Mexicans, so when you gon' make a move?"

"Need more intel. I want to hit them all, but that's not the way to go. I cannot let my emotions override my intellect."

"I hear you, but, damn, Boss man. But fuck that. We can still get at some of they ass."

"I agree, but I must make sure I hit the ones who murdered my family. If I start getting at them now, I lose my element of surprise."

Shaking his head, Cotton said, "No, you won't, Boss man. How will they know it's you? They won't. You got action at feeding your thirst for them Mexicans. I say we pounce on their ass."

As they returned to the car, Hot Shot let Cotton's words sink in. *Am I really thirsty? I have to keep control over my emotions, but he's right. I need to get this out of me.*

When they were on their way, Hot Shot turned toward Cotton and said, "You're right. So tonight, we make a move. See how many we can catch slipping. But I need to get the head of the I-13s. He's the one who gave the green light on my family. Anyone else along the way, as far as I'm concerned, is collateral damage."

Rubbing his hands together, Cotton said, "Now, *that's* what I'm talking about. Fuck these Mexicans. They got to get it."

"Right. Let's get back to the house. We got some planning to do."

"You know I'm with that, Boss man. What about Nola, though? She knows the business, but is her stomach strong enough to be a part of this?"

"I doubt it. She does want to be a part of this, but I can't let her. I cannot take the chance of something happening to her. I'll have to shake her. Come on; let's get back to the house while she's at the nail shop. Get your clothes ready."

"Bet."

They took my family, so I'm about to take as many of those bastards as I can. The I-13s don't know it, but they've turned Hot Shot into the Murder Man, and they won't even see him coming.

Hot Shot looked up toward the sky and said a silent prayer. *You know I love you, but I cannot let this slide. It's time to do the devil dance. Please, forgive me.*

Chapter Four

Hot Shot and Cotton were dressed in black army fatigues as they sat in a stolen SUV watching several Inglewood 13s as they were hanging outside of L.A. Tacos, a well-known Mexican restaurant on the Inglewood 13s' turf. Hot Shot surveyed the area to see what would be the best way to attack the gang members. He had to make sure they remained tactical. He couldn't afford to slip up; then everything would blow back on him and the mission, and he damn sure didn't want that to happen. JT would go nuts.

They were parked a block away from the gang members. Hot Shot thought they could just pull up in front of them and unload on them, but he scratched that thought. There were too many businesses around the restaurant, and that meant plenty of security cameras. Hot Shot was impatiently tapping the silenced 9 mm on his leg that he had in his hand as he continued to think. Cotton interrupted his thoughts.

"Boss man, no need to overthink this. Let's go park the truck around the corner from those fools, then creep up on their ass and give it to them—then bounce. We got these masks, so we get gooned up and move on they ass. For real, we can just pull in front of them, stop, and hop out on their ass."

"I thought about that, but there must be at least seven stores around them, and we can be spotted."

Shaking his head, Cotton said, "That shit won't matter. That's why we have the ski masks. As I said, you're overthinking this, Boss man. Let's go get they ass and get the fuck on."

Hot Shot thought about what Cotton said and agreed with him. He gave Cotton a nod and put the ski mask over his head, making sure his weapon was ready to fire. Cotton did the same, started the SUV, and pulled slowly from his parking place. When he stopped the SUV in front of the gang bangers, they jumped out, ran up on the group of Mexicans, and began shooting. The Mexicans were so shocked at what they saw they didn't have a chance to run. Hot Shot shot two in the head, then turned toward two more and quickly dropped them with two shots each to the head. Cotton got two Mexicans who tried to run. He shot them both in the back of their heads. Then he ran back to the SUV and watched as Hot Shot jumped inside, and they quickly sped away, leaving six Inglewood 13s dead in front of the restaurant.

They took off their ski masks as Cotton navigated the SUV back to where they parked Hot Shot's Audi. Neither said a word until Hot Shot pulled into his driveway.

"How do you feel, Boss man?" Cotton asked as he got out of the car.

"Honestly, I feel like I just took a sip of some delicious wine. I want more, though—much more."

"I feel you. Well, I'm out. I'm headed to Carson to scoop up this cutie. You need me, hit me."

They shook hands. Cotton left, and Hot Shot went inside the house, poured himself a drink, sat down on the sofa, and tried to relax. As he slowly calmed down, he wondered if he had turned into something he knew he wasn't. Did revenge give him justification to kill? Doing bad for the sake of doing good didn't justify what he and Cotton had just done. These thoughts pained him.

He stood to get another drink when he saw Nola staring at him from the top of the steps. She came down the stairs, saw what he was wearing, and knew he had done something.

"What you do, Shot?"

He stared at her for a few seconds and then said, "Handled some business."

"Are you okay? Because you look spooked."

"I'm good," he said as he downed his drink and made another.

"You lying. Your ass did something. You on your third drink, and you didn't even notice me as you came inside. I've been standing there watching you, and I can tell something is up. Talk to me."

She led him back to the sofa, and they sat down. He sighed and lay his head on Nola's shoulder. "We just got at some Mexicans from Inglewood 13. I feel messed about it."

"That's a normal feeling, baby. You need to relax and know that you did what you felt was right."

"What I did *wasn't* right, Nola. It was wrong. What I did goes against everything I stand for. The oath I swore when I got that badge, how I was raised—everything I believe in, I just went against it."

"Like I said, that's a normal feeling, especially for a man like you. You stand for right, and you just did wrong, and it's fucking with your head. You gotta shake that shit off if you're going to finish this, baby."

Shaking his head, he said, "That's not it at all, Nola. I feel totally opposite. I'm happy I did it, and I can't wait to do it again . . . and again. I want to kill as many as I can. It felt so satisfying each time I pulled the trigger. I want more. I *need* more, baby."

Damn, thought Nola as she held on to her man. "Oh, OK, well, you did the damn thing, and you feel conflicted, so what you gonna do?"

"Keep murdering the I-13s. Keep doing what I'm good at until I get as many of them as I can, and the ones I don't kill, I intend to have arrested. I know I'm in a dark place, and the only way I'll be able to see the light again is to get the people who killed my family."

"I understand, baby, and I know you will do what you need to do. But you can't torture yourself in the process. You must find a way to do this shit and maintain your sanity."

"Right. I'm worrying whether I'll be able to get to the light after everything is all said and done."

"You'll be able to bounce back easily because you're no cold-blooded killer. There's too much good inside of your heart. Now, come to bed with me and get some sleep. You need some rest, baby."

They went upstairs to the bedroom. Nola turned on the television while Hot Shot went into the bathroom to shower. When he finished, he felt a little better. Nola had the TV on the news, and just as she was about to change the channel, he stopped her.

"Wait, baby, I want to see something real quick."

The news anchorman came on the TV and began talking about the six murders that happened in the city of Inglewood.

I'm here at the gruesome murder scene here in Inglewood on North Arbor Vitae. Witnesses say they saw a dark-colored SUV pull in front of L.A. Tacos, and two men jumped out of it and began shooting, but no one heard any gunshots. That can only mean that the shooters had silenced weapons. They left six dead. Police on the scene say this looks as if it was gang related, perhaps the ongoing feud between the I-13s and the Lennox 13s or some of their other enemies. Either way, this was a massacre. The police are going to the nearby businesses to see if they can obtain any leads from their security cameras regarding this deadly murder scene. Hopefully, they'll be successful and make some arrests. This is Odell Littles reporting. Back to the studio.

Nola turned her head toward Hot Shot and said, "Damn, Shot. *Six* people? You went in hard as fuck, I see."

Shot stared at the TV and said, "Wish it would've been more for real."

"Were any of those six who you were looking for?"

He shrugged. "What I do know is there's much more to come their way."

"The newsman said two masked gunmen did that, so I assume that was you and your partner in crime, huh?"

"Yep."

"Where is that joker?"

"Gone over to some female's house."

"Figures. Well, you've started off with a bang, mister."

"You think?" he replied sarcastically.

"What do you think JT will say about this?"

"Why would he say something to me about what happened to those Mexicans?"

"Oh, I'd say when he hears about six Inglewood 13s murdered by two gunmen who had silenced weapons, he'll pretty much be giving you a call, buddy," she said with her words dripping with sarcasm.

Before Hot Shot could respond to his wife . . . his cell phone started ringing. He groaned when he grabbed it and saw JT's name on the incoming screen. Nola saw JT's name as well and started laughing.

Hot Shot sent the call to voicemail, hoping JT would wait until tomorrow to give him hell. However, his hopes were in vain because his phone started ringing again. He answered this time.

"You *do* know you need to have your ass at my house first thing in the morning, right? No, scratch that shit. *I'll* be at *your* house in the morning. Make sure the entire team is there," screamed JT as he ended the call without giving Hot Shot a chance to speak.

Nola heard everything because of JT's screaming. "Looks like hell is about to be raised here in the morning. I got an early hair appointment, so I won't be here for that shit."

Shaking his head, Hot Shot said, "You heard the man. He wants the *entire* team here. That includes you, lady."

"No way. I'm not in that mess."

Laughing, Hot Shot got comfortable on the bed and said, "Yes, my love, you are. Good night."

"Ugh." She then whacked her husband with her pillow, and they both laughed.

Chapter Five

The following day, Hot Shot was downstairs finishing his daily workout when he heard JT's truck pull into his driveway. He grabbed his towel and began drying off as he went to let JT inside. "Here we go," he said as he opened the door for JT.

"You are going to wind up being in the cell right next door to the fucking criminals you've helped put in there," JT yelled as he walked past Hot Shot, then turned around, fuming, and continued. "Where is your partner in crime and your loving wife? Get them down here so I can make myself perfectly fucking clear on what I'm about to tell y'all."

Hot Shot had never seen JT this mad, so he chose to wait before responding to how he felt. Instead, he went upstairs and woke both Nola and Cotton. When he returned downstairs, JT was at the bar having a drink. Hot Shot grinned and said, "You're drinking this early in the morning because you're upset. I get that, but you need to calm down, JT. Yelling your head off isn't going to change what happened. To be honest with you, nothing you can say to me will change how I feel and how I intend to move forward. You, of all people, should understand how I'm getting down with this mission. This is more than a mission; this is personal, *very* personal. And the only way I will stop is when I find the Mexicans who murdered my family and the top man of their gang who gave the order to have my family slaughtered like animals."

JT poured another drink and calmly spoke. "Son, you're right. I understand, but the law is the law, and you are working under federal law. That doing some bad to do some good applies *only* to the mission. You can't get all vigilante with this shit. That shit was on every fucking news channel, son. That type of attention is exactly what we *can't* have." Before Hot Shot could speak, Nola and Cotton came downstairs and spoke to him.

"Okay, now that the entire team is here, I'm going to address this serious concern, and I promise you, we will never have this type of conversation again. What was done last night cannot and *will not* happen again. Now, anything that has to happen during the mission . . . then so be it. What you two did last night was cold-blooded murder, and it was fucking caught on four different security cams. Cotton, the only reason I can't arrest your ass right now is that this joker is involved, and his involvement protects you . . . of sorts. Don't think for one second I won't hang your ass out to dry if some more stupid shit like this goes down."

Then JT glared at Nola.

Nola smiled and said, "I knew nothing about this, JT. I found out last night after the fact."

"Take that damn smile off your face, lady. You may be innocent *this* time, but I'm warning you so you won't make any future mistakes by joining your husband's dumb-ass ideas."

Nola's smile turned to a frown, and Hot Shot dropped his head because this team meeting was about to get ugly.

"JT, you're the captain of the team, so your authority will not be questioned by me, but I will *not* tolerate any form of disrespect toward me or my husband. What Hot Shot did, he did based on his emotions. So, we'll address that and move accordingly. I hear you, but you need to respect us even when you're upset."

"Before I continue, do you have anything *you* want to say, Cotton?"

Hot Shot felt Nola's words were relatively calm, and he was relieved. However, he didn't know what to expect from Cotton.

"Yeah, I got something to say, JT. I'm rolling with my man however he chooses to get down—right, wrong, or whatever. If you gon' lock me down for that, then so be it because that *won't* change."

"What about you, son? Do you have anything to add to this team meeting?" JT asked sarcastically.

Hot Shot smiled and said, "You know how I feel, but I will look at things in a broader sense before I do what I choose to do. Remember, you and the director gave me *plenty of room* to handle each mission."

"Correct. 'Mission' is the key word, son. The damn mission doesn't say that you can commit any damn gang-style killing on the damn streets of Inglewood. Push me if you want to, son, and I'll have all your asses in a fucking federal prison. Do what you must, son, but just control yourself and your feelings." JT sighed. "Okay, I've spoken my piece, and I've listened to each of you. Are we on the same page?"

Each person nodded.

"With that out of the way, who wants breakfast? I'm starving," Nola asked as she headed toward the kitchen. "JT, your ass needs to put down that liquor and put something on your stomach."

They all started laughing.

Hot Shot had the weapons and was ready to deliver them to the Inglewood 13s. He made the call to Termite. When Termite answered, Hot Shot said, "I'm ready to see you. This is how we're going to move. In thirty minutes, I need Toker to meet my man in the parking lot of Sentinel Field. When my man tells me he has the money, I'll pull up to Hillcrest Continuation and drop off your purchase."

"That's cool, homes," Termite said and ended the call.

Hot Shot pulled into the driveway and went inside to see Cotton and Nola sitting in the living room. "It's time to dance, Cotton. Go to the spot I told you about and wait for Toker. Once you get the money, Toker is not to leave until you count the money. Understood?

"You know I got it, Boss man," Cotton said as he stood and left the house.

Hot Shot saw that his wife was dressed in loose-fitting sweatpants with a matching hoodie. He started shaking his head. "No, Nola. You are *not* going with me to handle this business."

Nola laughed as she stood and exited the house and got inside of the black Denali Hot Shot had rented for the drop-off.

"Then again, I guess you *are* coming along with me."

Once inside the SUV, he reached in the glove box, pulled out a compact 9 mm, and gave the gun to his wife. He watched her as she checked to ensure the chamber had a loaded round inside, then set the gun on her lap.

"You are not to leave the truck, Nola. Watch my six, that's it. If anything looks shady, you will know, then move."

Nola turned up the music on her phone as one of the rapper Tech N9ne's songs started playing. She bobbed her head up and down, totally ignoring her husband's orders. Hot Shot just shook his head.

"You're going to have to listen to me on this stuff, Nola, or you will not be a part of the business," he said in a firm tone.

Too firm for Nola's taste. "I heard what you said, Jason. As for you not letting me be a part of the get down—humph. I wish you would just *try* to stop me."

"Oh, I can, and I will, Nola. This isn't a game. It's serious, and I don't want you in harm's way. You need to listen to me and do as I ask."

"See, that's better, how you ask me. That, I can deal with, but all the barking orders—that I *won't* deal with. I understand this is not a game. I may be a country girl, but I know how to handle shit."

"OK. I apologize, but this is the first time you're in the business, and I cannot help but worry, baby. If something happened to you, I'd die."

Nola placed her left hand on Hot Shot's right thigh and sighed. "I know, baby. That's why I'll listen to you, my big FBI man." This relaxed him as he smiled and continued driving toward Inglewood's north side.

Hot Shot called Cotton to see if everything was kosher with him and Toker.

"Yeah, I'm good, Boss man. The count is on point."

"OK, let him roll out, and I want you to bend the corner and park behind my vehicle. Once I'm out of the truck, you come and start unloading the weapons."

"Gotcha," Cotton said and ended the call.

"Here we go, baby. Remember, remain cool and watch my six. Everything should go smoothly. If it doesn't, you'll know what to do," Hot Shot said as he pulled in front of Hillcrest Continuation and parked the SUV.

He climbed out of the truck and strolled casually toward Termite and Puma. The gang members wore their typical *vato* stances, looking like they were the hardest gangsters in the world. Hot Shot wanted to beat the hell out of them but controlled that urge. So instead, he smiled and said, "All is well, gentlemen. You care to come look at the merchandise?"

"No fucking doubt, homes," Termite said as he led the way back toward Hot Shot's SUV.

"We don't normally let our money move without us, so I sure hope this shit is on the up-and-up. Any funny shit, then it's your ass, Mr. Hot Shot," said Puma.

"I play no games. I'm very serious about my business. I would have agreed to a straight-up exchange, but that 'rob me' statement changed the rules. Anyway, that's a moot point now." Hot Shot opened the rear door of the SUV and let the two Mexican gang members check out their purchase.

When Cotton pulled up behind them, the two gang members turned around and instantly began reaching for their weapons.

"Whoa, now, gentlemen. It's all good. That's my man here to help us unload the cargo."

"We don't need no damn help. Tell him to stay in his fucking car, or I'm blastin', homes," Puma said in a menacing tone.

Hot Shot held up his hands, stopping Cotton from getting out of his truck. He turned back toward the SUV. "You can continue, gentlemen." The two men went back to surveying the weapons.

Termite told Hot Shot, "Looks good, homes. We might be getting right back at you for more firepower. Shit is about to get crazy in Inglewood."

Puma gave his brother a look that could kill and then told him, "Let's get these boxes loaded up, homes."

Hot Shot assisted in loading the weapons in the back of the Mexicans' Dodge Ram. When they had packed all the boxes, Hot Shot said, "There you go, gentlemen. If you need to get at me again, I'm around. If you know anyone else who needs weapons, be sure to throw me some business, and I'll cut the prices for you."

"Yeah, we just might do that. But like my brother said, we may get back to you soon."

"That's fine with me."

They shook hands, and Hot Shot returned to his vehicle.

"All is well now. We can go home and chill," Hot Shot told Nola as he started the SUV.

"For a minute there, I thought I was going to have to blow those Mexicans' heads off."

"Nah, it's all good. Cotton just spooked the hell outta them."

"I saw that. Now, tell me, how does this shit work with these Mexicans? You sold them guns, I see, but how will you get them?"

"Each gun they bought has a small tracking device, so JT will know wherever they're located. Then, in a few days, he'll send in the good guys to raid the location where the guns are being held."

"That simple, huh?"

"Yep."

"It would seem to me that with a good mouthpiece, they could beat the case. I mean, how will JT be able to get a search warrant to justify the raid?"

"Glad to see you up on the law, but it doesn't work that way with all raids. JT will call in a tip about the weapons, and Inglewood PD will move on that with an impromptu warrant. And that, my loving wife, is how we get down. We just done some bad to do some good, as JT likes to say."

"That's some corny country talk for real. OK, I got that part, but what is *your* plan? How are we going to get turned up on those Mexicans? Especially with JT on our ass so damn tough?"

"That, my loving wife, is something I'm still trying to figure out."

Chapter Six

Cotton was lying on the couch watching TV while talking to one of his many female friends, but he sat up suddenly and told his friend that he would call her back, then yelled for Nola and Hot Shot to come downstairs. He grabbed the remote control for the television, turned up the volume, and listened as the news reporter reported some breaking news. Hot Shot and Nola joined him and watched the news wearing smiles.

The reporter said, "Early this morning, the Inglewood Police gang task force raided two homes where several members of the Inglewood 13s, a well-known Hispanic gang in the city of Inglewood, lived. Authorities say they retrieved a large number of drugs and guns, making this one of the largest drug and gun busts in the city of Inglewood."

Then the reporter called out to the head detective for an interview. "Detective Sanchez, can you give our viewers any details about this raid?"

"Acting on a tip we received, we raided two homes on the north side of Inglewood and found more guns and drugs than we've ever confiscated in one raid. It proves that the Inglewood 13s, a Hispanic gang here in our city, are as dangerous as we've always known. Hopefully, today's success will hurt the gang's finances from their ill-gotten gains from the drug trade. We're incredibly proud of the fact that we've taken so many guns off the streets. We've saved lives today, hurt the gang financially, and taken many of their weapons."

The reporter ended, "There you have it. Chalk up one for the good guys. Back to you, Jim."

Smiling, Hot Shot said, "Now, let's see how long it will take for Toker to get at me."

"What makes you think he'll call?" asked Cotton.

Before Hot Shot could answer, Nola said, "They most likely lost all the guns they just bought. And with those raids being televised, they will have to get back quickly before their enemies pounce on their ass."

Hot Shot smiled at his wife and said, "Correct. We've taken a few of their soldiers off the street as well. We'll take even more of them off the streets when they get back at me."

"Fuck puttin' them wetbacks in jail. When we gon' murk some more of them bitches for killin' your family, Boss man?"

"When the time is right, you already know we'll make our move."

"The move needs to be done right, Shot. We cannot afford to piss off JT again. That man was smoking hot," Nola said as she stared at her man.

Hot Shot understood what she meant by the statement and knew it was twofold. Nola was worried if they made JT mad, he wouldn't give her the green light to talk to or visit her sister. He grabbed his wife's hand and led her upstairs.

"I don't want you to worry about being able to get at Lola, baby." He grabbed his phone and gave it to his wife. "Give her a call and let her know you're home and out here with me."

"She's going to be asking me crazy questions, baby."

"I know she will. Tell her that you will explain everything to her in time. You're calling to let her know you're home and you're safe."

"Now, you know that's going to drive her nuts."

"It's your decision, Nola. I know you need to speak to her. This is the only way we can move right now."

"Did JT give you the go-ahead for this, Shot?"

"No. I need you to focus on us and everything we're doing, and the longer you go without talking to your twin sister, the harder it will be on you. So make the call," he said as he turned and went back downstairs to give his wife some privacy while she called her twin.

Tears slid down Nola's face as she dialed her sister's number. When Lola answered the phone, Nola said, "Hey, sister, how are you doing?"

Lola smiled as she said, "Girl, I know your ass ain't got no damn cell phone in that place. You're trying to get some more time added to what you got?"

"Relax, I'm out, Lola."

"You what?"

"You heard me. I'm out."

"When the hell did that happen? How did that happen? Where the fuck are you?" Lola asked rapidly.

Laughing, Nola lied, "I came home a few days ago. I can't really go into all the details. Just know I'm out here in sunny California with my husband."

"You with Hot Shot? Wait a minute. You have to tell me how all this shit happened, Nola. For real? What the fuck is going on?"

"I will, but right now, I'm enjoying myself with Hot Shot. I'm sorry I didn't get right at you, but a bitch been horny as fuck. All I've been doing is having great sex and eating."

Shaking her head in disbelief, Lola said, "I know that's right, but I still want to know how you got out. You didn't run off from that place, Nola, did you?"

"Hell no. Trust me, I'll get to you with everything later. I'm home, and that's all that matters. Have you heard from bro and our cousins?"

"Yeah, they're good. You know Troy always calling, having me call different females on three-way so he can run his game on them. Keeta Wee and Weeta Wee call me once a week. They're good too."

"OK, cool. Tell them I send love, and I'll have a number for them to call me too. OK, girl, let me get off this phone. When I get a phone, I'll send you the number. If you need me, call me on this number. It's Hot Shot's phone."

"OK. Nola, I'm glad you're home. I missed you so much. I can never repay you for what you did for me. I love you, sister."

"I love you too. It is what it is. I couldn't let you go to jail. I knew you wouldn't have made it. It's all good. But I'm still mad at you for what you did, Lola. Your freaky ass just couldn't help yourself. You just had to fuck Hot Shot. Again, it is what it is."

"I'm sorry, sister. I know I was wrong. Please forgive me," Lola said sincerely, tears sliding down her cheeks.

"I forgive you. Now, let me go, and I'll give you a call in a day or so. Bye-bye," Nola said and ended the call with tears on her cheeks as well. She sat down on the bed and continued to cry tears of happiness. Everything was going to be all right. She was home, she spoke to her sister, her husband was right by her side, and it was definitely all good. *Thank you, Lord,* she prayed silently.

Hot Shot and Cotton had just finished their workout for the morning. Both were sweating from their morning regimen of push-ups, sit-ups, jumping jacks, and stretches. Hot Shot finally got Cotton on board with the early-morning workout. Cotton fought it as long as he could, then finally gave in. Now that he'd gotten used to the workout, it felt good, just like Hot Shot told him it would.

"Proud of you, Cotton. You're handling the workout just fine. Time for us to go up to 1,500 of everything we do. You with that?"

"I'm just now getting used to this 1,000 push-ups, sit-ups, and all the rest of this shit you got me doing every morning. Come on, Boss man, let me make it."

Laughing, Hot Shot said, "Don't worry. You'll be all right. It's all about building up to do more, and you've progressed well enough to step it up some." The ringing of his cell phone stopped Hot Shot. He grabbed his phone and smiled. "It's Toker."

"Damn, y'all said he would be hitting, but you didn't think it would be this fast. Nola was on point."

"Yep," said Hot Shot as he answered his phone. "What's good, Toker?"

"We need to talk. A lot of shit has gone down, and we need to meet ASAP."

"Talk to me."

"Can't right now. Puma and Termite are in jail along with a gang of my homies and homegirls. We got it bad and lost all of what we got from you."

"Whoa, that's a big hit."

"Right. Check it; we need to meet up. Since Puma and Termite are on lock, you'll meet Franco today. He doesn't want me to handle it alone, so you get to meet the top dog."

"Good, very good. When and where?"

"Fatburgers on the corner of Crenshaw and Manchester. One hour."

"I'll be there," Hot Shot said and ended the call thinking about how fortunate he was since he was about to meet the top dog of the I-13s . . . The man who gave the green light for his family to be executed. The man he wanted just as bad as the other Mexicans who actually killed his family. He felt his anger swell and took a few deep breaths to calm himself. He had to have control of his emotions. It would be hard not to blow this Franco guy's brains out once he was face-to-face. Hot Shot shook his head. No, Franco was going to die slowly.

"You okay, Boss man?"

Hot Shot smiled at his right-hand man and said, "Yes, I'm real good, Cotton. I'm about to go real quick. I'm meeting Toker and some other Mexicans in an hour."

"You need me to roll with you?"

"No, I got it. It's going to be quick in and out."

"Okay, I'm about to get showered then go fuck with this bitch out in Lynwood."

"You need to be careful, Cotton. You're messing with too many different females out here. That can be dangerous. These California women are known for being shiesty."

"I feel you, Boss man, but I'm good."

"OK."

Hot Shot went upstairs, got dressed, and was out the door. He pulled into the parking lot of the Fatburger's restaurant ten minutes ahead of schedule. Then he got out of his car and went inside the 7-Eleven in the same parking lot as Fatburgers. He bought a pack of gum, stepped outside the store, and watched Toker as he pulled into the parking lot and parked next to his car. Immediately, he stepped to Toker's side of the vehicle.

"What it do, Toker?"

"It's all bad right now. Hop in, and let's bend a corner and chop it up." Hot Shot got into the backseat, and Toker pulled out of the parking lot. "Hot Shot, this is Franco. Franco, this is Hot Shot."

Franco was a dark-skinned Mexican with many gang tattoos all over his body, face included. *So, this is the top dog,* Hot Shot said to himself.

"Nice to meet you."

"Same here, homes. We need to get the same load we already got from you. We lost all that firepower we purchased a couple of weeks ago," Franco said as he kept his eyes straight ahead, not making any eye contact with Hot Shot.

"That won't be a problem. The ticket will be the same unless you want more."

"No, the same is good. It's 140,000, right?"

"Yes. When you want to make it happen?"

"How long will it take for you to get everything ready?"

"I'll make the call and get back to you later."

"Can you make the call now? We need these weapons like yesterday, homes," Franco said in a serious tone.

Hot Shot pulled out his phone and called JT. When JT answered, Hot Shot got straight to the point. "I need the same order I made a few weeks ago."

"For the same people?" asked JT.

"Yes. When can you have everything ready for me?"

"Someone with you right now, son?"

"Yes."

"I can have everything by the end of the week. Will that suffice?"

"Hold on," Hot Shot said as he put the phone on his lap and asked Franco, "Is the end of the week cool with you?" Franco nodded his head. Hot Shot then put the phone back to his ear and said, "Yes, that will do."

"Cool. Give me a call when you can talk," JT said and ended the call.

Toker made a U-turn and headed back toward Fatburgers.

"We will do it like we did last time, Toker. Will that be cool?"

"No, it won't," answered Franco. "We have to move differently with this shipment. Too many of my people are gone, and I want to make sure that not many people will know the business. So when you're ready for us, I'll have Toker get at you where we will meet up to make it happen. Is that cool with you, homes?"

"I don't have a problem with that. Just as long as no games will be played."

Franco turned in his seat, so Hot Shot could see him and said, "I don't play games, homes."

Hot Shot nodded his understanding just as Toker parked his car next to Hot Shot's Audi.

"Okay, then, I'll hit you once I have everything in my hand, and we'll proceed from there."

"That's right," Franco said in a dismissing tone.

Hot Shot got out of Toker's car without saying anything else. He got in his car and exhaled loudly. His hands were trembling so badly that he knew not to start his car. He had wanted to reach up and grab Franco by his neck and choke the shit out of the Mexican until he was no longer breathing. The temptation had been so strong that he literally had to beg himself to remain calm. Tears slid down his face slowly as he sat in his car. He knew he was going to murder Franco. No way was he letting that man go to jail, and that thought calmed him as he sat in his car thinking about his father, mother, and little brother. Damn.

Chapter Seven

Cotton was sitting inside his truck, waiting for the female he'd met online. She was super sexy to him, so he had to set up a meeting. That Facebook dating shit had him meeting all types of California bitches. He hoped and prayed that she looked as good in person as she did on her profile page, he thought as he sat in his truck smoking a blunt. He smiled when he saw her coming out of her house, so he tapped his horn, and she turned his way. He watched as she walked slowly toward his truck, and the way she walked seemed as if she were gliding on air. Cotton got out of his vehicle, stepped to her, and hugged her.

"Mmm, you look good, and you smell good. Damn, you put your profile to shame."

"Thank you. You're so sweet," she replied as he opened his truck and pulled the step ladder down so she could climb inside. "This is a huge truck. It's going to be fun riding in this."

"Trust me, Yolanda, you will definitely enjoy the ride."

They both laughed as Cotton went around to the driver's side of his truck, wondering if she caught the double entendre he slipped on her.

Hot Shot and Nola were at the grocery store picking up things for Nola to cook. She said the kitchen didn't have the necessary items for a woman to be able to prepare proper meals. So she dragged him to Ralph's Grocery Store, and he couldn't believe how much of everything she was buying.

"Baby, don't you think we have enough food now? I mean, we already have this shopping cart full. How much more you got to get?"

"Just a few more things, baby. Stop whining. This is what married couples do. This is our family time."

He smiled but said to himself, *I'd rather be watching the Lakers.* Then to his wife, he said, "That's right, dear."

Nola caught his sarcasm, stopped, and punched his arm. "Boy, you don't want to piss me off. Family time is important to me. My mother and father used to go to the grocery store together all the time. It's a bonding thing, Shot."

Knowing how much she missed and loved her deceased parents, he grabbed her and said, "I'm with you, baby, now and forever. No matter how much bonding family time you need, I got you."

She smiled and said, "Family time also entails hot, sweaty sex after a good meal." She winked and added a slight sway to her thick hips as she walked before him. He smiled and thought, *Thank God for family time.*

After a nice dinner at Tequila Jacks at the Long Beach Pike, Cotton drove to the beach, and they walked and talked and got to know each other better. They watched as the sun set, then headed back to the truck because he became chilly from the Pacific breeze.

"I enjoyed myself, Cotton. I hope this won't be the only time we go out."

"No way, baby. I'm really trying to get to know you better. I'm feeling you, gurl," he said, his words dripping with his Texas drawl.

"Good. I'm feeling you too. You know what I really like about you, Cotton?"

"What, baby?"

"I hope this won't offend you."

"No worries."

"I love the way you talk. It sounds country but kinda sexy."

Cotton laughed and said, "So, here I thought it was my Mack Daddy vibe I was giving, and it was my Texas sound you digging, huh? It's cool, girl, because once you get with a Texan, you'll never want anything else. You know what they say in Texas, right?"

She giggled and said, "What?"

He couldn't believe she fell for his joke and said, "Everything is big in Texas."

She laughed so hard tears slid down her cheeks. Then finally, she wiped her eyes and said in a low, seductive voice, "If that means what I *think* it means, what I think it does, then I guess I *will* be enjoying that ride."

In the heaviest Southern drawl he could muster, Cotton said, "Ooh wee, gurl. You sho' in fa the ride of yer life." They both laughed as he helped her up the ladder back inside his truck, making sure he got a little squeeze of her backside this time.

She got in the seat and tried to imitate him by saying, "All right there, pa'tna, squeezing this ass will get you in a world of trouble."

Cotton laughed, got inside the truck, and replied, "Gurl, this here Texan is built for all types of trouble." Though he was playing, he didn't realize that trouble was about to come his way. Since Yolanda stayed just a few minutes from the beach, Cotton had her home in ten minutes. He got out of the truck and helped her out. He was feeling Yolanda and was thinking this could possibly be his Nola. He admired what Hot Shot had with Nola and wanted the same . . . some real love. He quickly shook that thought out of his mind. No fucking way will he ever let love for a woman in his heart ever again.

Yolanda was five foot three, weighing 165, and drop-dead gorgeous, but she wasn't that good-looking enough to ever make him renege on his vow never to love a woman again. What happened to his true love, Meosha, made him vow never to let love in his heart again. It pained him to even think about the brutal rape his girlfriend had to endure, all because of him and the life he led in the streets of Dallas, Texas. A rape so terrible that Meosha took her own life right in front of him. It had been almost three years ago, but the very thought of that night made it feel as if it were yesterday. *Nope, no love for me. I gotta stick to the script and stick and hit,* he thought and smiled as they reached Yolanda's front door.

Yolanda turned toward him and kissed him, making him feel he was being seduced by a porn star. The way her soft, small tongue swirled around inside his mouth made him moan.

The kiss ended, and Cotton said, "Damn, gurl, what was that?"

Before she could answer, her eyes grew wide, and she said, "Damn, here comes my son's father."

Cotton turned around and saw a tall, slim brother with long braids, and he couldn't help but think he was the rapper Snoop Dog. I mean, hey, they were in the city of LBC. Cotton could tell by the look on Snoop Dog's face that this great night was about to go all bad. *Fuck. I left my fucking gun in the truck,* he said to himself just as Snoop Dog stood in front of him and Yolanda.

"Bitch, what I tell you about having niggas in around my son?"

Yolanda showed no fear when she replied, "Doug, you better go on with that bullshit. You just trying to start some shit. You ain't paying no bills, so you can't tell me shit. Dante is at my mama's house anyway, so you need to kill that shit. And if I'm a bitch, *you* a bitch."

"So. you gon' act tough in front of this ho-ass nigga? Bitch, I'll slap the shit outta you *and* this bitch-ass nigga." Doug glared at Cotton with a look that was daring Cotton to say something—anything.

There was nothing soft about Cotton, and he knew he could fuck up Doug's lightweight ass. But he noticed once Doug got loud, three more Crip-looking dudes got out of Doug's SUV. *Fuck,* he thought. Now he realized it could go *all* bad, so he acted as if he was totally ignoring Doug while he pulled out his phone. But what he really was doing was texting Hot Shot, letting him know he needed him.

Need you, Boss man. Looks like I'm about to get jumped by some Crips. Hurry!

Hot Shot responded in less than a minute and texted back. Is your locator on?

Cotton responded. Yep.

Hot Shot texted back. On my way. ETA 17 minutes.

Relieved, Cotton knew he just had to buy himself some time, so he told Doug, "Check it out, brother. There's no need for all the disrespect. I understand this is your son's mom, and I'm in no way trying to disrespect you. We went out on a friendly date, that's it. That's all."

Doug stuck out his skinny chest, taking Cotton's words for weakness, and said, "Look, nigga, I'm not trying to hear that soft-ass shit. I suggest you get to stepping before you get fucked up in these Long Beach streets, cuh."

Hearing Cotton sounding like a weak nigga had Yolanda looking at him like . . . *Damn shame. I liked this nigga.* There was no way in hell she could fuck with a spineless nigga.

"Look, Doug, he doesn't want problems with you, so you need to quit that shit. The only reason you poppin' that shit is because you got your homeboys with your ass."

"Bitch, you got me twisted. I'll give this nigga a fair fade on Crip."

"Yeah, whatever. You know damn well I know how you get down. Once he got to beating that ass, your homeboys will jump in. Knock it off."

There you go, baby, keep talking, Cotton said as he checked his phone and saw that Hot Shot had texted him.

ETA 5 minutes.

Cotton couldn't help but smile because this situation was about to turn in his favor. He couldn't wait because he wanted to beat the fuck out of loud-ass-mouth Doug.

"Again, brother, I don't want any problems with you. But you really need to miss me with the aggression."

Cotton's words shocked Doug. "Oh, so Mister Friendly is *kinda* tough, huh? All right, cuh, this what we gon' do. We gon' get on this grass and go head up, and on Long Beach Crip, my homies won't jump in. Just me and you, cuh. What's up?"

Cotton saw Hot Shot's Audi and smiled. "You really don't want that, Doug, but you gon' get it because I didn't care to be called a bitch and a ho. Ain't none of that makeup in my DNA."

Yolanda smiled and thought, *OK, baby, that's my Texan.*

Hot Shot and Nola jumped out of the Audi and stepped past the three Crips as if they weren't standing there. When they got next to Cotton, Hot Shot said, "Let's go, Cotton."

"Who the fuck is this nigga, cuh?" asked Doug.

Cotton smiled because he knew what was coming next.

Hot Shot turned toward Doug and said, "My name is Hot Shot, and I would appreciate it if you didn't use that N-word in my presence."

Doug turned toward his homeboys, who came closer and said, "Cuh, you hear this corny-ass nigga?" Then before he knew what happened, Hot Shot slapped Doug so hard it looked like one of his braids flew off his head.

The three Crips looked as if they were about to advance on Hot Shot, and Nola quickly pulled out her 9 mm and said, "I really don't think you guys want this. Now, come on, Cotton. We out."

Shaking his head, he pointed at Doug and said, "No, Nola. This dude put it on Crip he would give me a fair one, and I want that fade." He stepped on the grass and told a dazed Doug, "Come, tough Crip, shake that off and come get this head up."

Yolanda laughed so hard that everyone turned and stared at her. "Go on, cuh, go get that fade."

Knowing he couldn't lose face in front of his homeboys, Doug reluctantly stepped onto the grass.

"Yeah, cuh, I want that fade on Crip." Then with lightning-fast speed, Cotton hit Doug three times. Two hard body shots and a right uppercut dropped Doug on his ass, out like the count.

Pumped, he said, "Damn, this is what you Crips are like out here? Texas Crips are tougher than you drive-by-ass fools." He aimed the insult at the other three Crips to see if they would bite. They didn't. They were too focused on Nola, who had lowered her weapon but still had it out, tapping it lightly on her thigh.

"Say goodbye to your friend, and let's go, Cotton. Fun over with," Hot Shot said as he and Nola started walking toward the car.

Looking at Doug still knocked out on the grass kind of made Yolanda feel sorry for him. *Fuck him,* she thought as she wrapped her arms around Cotton and gave him another one of those seductive kisses and said, "Make sure you call me when you get home, my sexy Texan."

Cotton smiled his pearly whites at her and said, "No doubt, baby gurl. When dude wakes up, tell him he got what he wanted, and if he ever wants some more, he can get it too."

Laughing, she said, "Fuck him." Then she turned to Doug's homies and said, "Y'all need to get your friend up and get the fuck on."

Cotton turned and walked past the Crips, got into his truck, and pulled off. He was laughing all the way home. But he knew when he got there, he was about to be scolded by both Hot Shot and Nola. But fuck, it wasn't his fault. However, he knew what was coming as he pulled into the driveway. Fuck . . .

Chapter Eight

Hot Shot wasn't angry with Cotton; he was worried. Cotton didn't understand that living in Southern California was much different. These L.A. streets can get a person hurt really easily. One had to always stay on their toes and take nothing for granted. So when Cotton came into the house looking like he was about to get scolded, Hot Shot smiled.

"It's all good, Cotton. I told you these streets are different out here. All you did was go over to a female's house and look at what almost happened."

"I feel you, Boss man. I mean, we had a chill evening. Then I brought Yolanda home, and the baby daddy showed up tripping. I was really slipping because I had left my pistol in the truck. Otherwise, I would've handled the situation my way."

"I'm glad it went the way it did. Don't need you catching a case out here. But you need to vet these females more in-depth to make sure there's no baby daddy or anything extra in her life. I can't stress to you how crazy it is out here. But again, it's all good. I'm about to go lay it down for the night. You straight?"

"Yeah, I'm good, Boss man. I feel you, though, did you see how bad that bitch is?"

Shaking his head, Hot Shot laughed and said, "You are special, Cotton, real special. See you in the morning."

Cotton still was laughing as Hot Shot went upstairs, relieved that Hot Shot wasn't mad at him. He pulled out his phone and called Yolanda. "Hey you, you good?"

"Yes, baby, I'm straight. I'm sorry you had to go through all that mess with my son's father. He be on that stupid shit like we're still together."

"No worries, baby. I'm sure he realized his mistake tonight."

"I know, right? When your homeboy slapped the shit out of him, I could've died laughing. Then when you beat him up so fast, it made it funnier."

"I didn't want to take it there, but he kept pushing and pushing until I had enough. That's why I hit my people to ensure we'd be safe."

"That was smart. I won't front. I was kinda disappointed in you at first; thought you were scared."

"I only fear God, baby gurl. I left my pistol in the truck, and the way his friends were looking, I knew the odds were against me, so I texted my people."

"That female wasn't no joke. She whipped that gun out, and by the look in her eyes, I could tell she wasn't on no faking shit. She was with the bullshit for real."

"Yep. Nola doesn't play any games. Anyway, we can put that behind us. I'm trying to see you again."

"I'm with that. When you wanna hook up, baby?"

"ASAP. You let me know when you're free, and I'll make it happen."

"OK. I'd rather meet you this time, just in case my ex be on some lurking shit."

"That's cool because I'd hate to make your son fatherless."

Yolanda could tell he was serious, and that excited her. But even though she was not with Doug now, she didn't want anything to happen to him. After all, he was still her son's dad. "Facts. OK, baby, I'll call you tomorrow."

"Indeed. Good night, baby."

"Good night." Yolanda ended the call smiling as she called her best friend back so she could finish telling her about the night she had with Cotton.

After Cotton hung up the phone, he took a shower and got in bed, thinking about how he picked a winner by hooking up with Yolanda. He grabbed his phone and started surfing through Facebook dating, looking for another winner. He loved these California women. As he swiped, he saw a female that looked tasty and quickly hit the heart and hoped this one would respond because she looked sexy. Then he closed his phone, turned on the TV, and watched some of *The First 48* until he fell asleep.

The next morning after they finished their workout, Hot Shot got the call from JT that he would have everything he needed for the I-13s in two days. Hot Shot then called Toker and told him he would be ready for them in a couple of days. Toker told him that that was cool because Franco had been really uneasy since those raids.

"It's all good. He'll have what he wants. *You* good, though?"

"Yeah, I'm the only person Franco trusts because he knows there's a snitch, so he's not trying to trust anyone but me because I didn't know anything about the guns and dope or where they were. So that put me in good with him. But, man, if he ever finds out that *I'm* the one, he'd really fuck me off."

"You don't have to worry. We're solid. You make sure you keep yourself out of the way so that when everything goes down again, he'll continue to think it's someone else who's in the business. That way, he will trust you even more."

"Facts. All right, I'm about to get at Franco now."

"Stay safe, Toker."

"Bet," Toker said and ended the call.

Hot Shot went upstairs and saw Nola was on the phone, so he took off his clothes and got in the shower. When he finished, he entered the bedroom and saw Nola had ended her phone conversation and was sitting on the bed, deep in thought.

"What's good, baby?"

"I'm missing my sister, Shot. I need to go see her soon."

"I understand, baby. We can make that happen."

"I knew you would say that, baby. Thank you, but I'm not trying to go right now. You need me here to watch your six. So Lola will have to wait."

Laughing, Hot Shot told his wife, "Baby, I've been doing this shit a minute now. So you don't have to worry about me. I got this."

Shaking her head, she told him. "No, you don't. If this business was the normal stuff you do, I wouldn't worry. But this is too personal for you, and letting your emotions control your moves will serve up a bad situation. So I got to stand by you to make sure you control those reckless emotions."

He stared at his wife, not wanting to admit she was right. He loved her so much. She was his rider for real, and he was so grateful she was by his side. Yet, he had to do what he had to do, and that was to take Franco's life. He also needed to know exactly who killed his family. Yes, Franco made the call to do it. For that, his death was imminent, but he needed to get the shooters too. Then and only then will he feel his quench for murder satisfied. Those Mexicans killed his immediate family, and for that, their lives were his to take. Period.

Chapter Nine

Hot Shot really didn't care for Nola's twin sister, Lola. She tricked him by pretending to be her twin and had sex with him. That was so scandalous that he had never cared for her since then. But she was his wife's sister, and he would never interfere with their bond. That's why he was picking up Lola from the airport so she could reunite with her twin sister.

Hot Shot saw her as she exited the airport. He blew his horn, and Lola saw him and started walking toward his car. He jumped out of his vehicle, took her bags, put them in the trunk, and then got back inside, purposely not opening the door for her. She hopped inside the car and smiled.

"Hi, Hot Shot."

"Hey," he said as he eased his car into the heavy LAX traffic.

"Thank you for sending for me so I can visit with my sister. I can't wait to hug her neck."

"No problem. Nola really needs to see you, and there's nothing I won't do for her."

"I respect that about you. I know how much you love my sister. I'm sorry for what I did. I was dead wrong for sexing you. Please, forgive me. No excuse. I just wanted to see how good your sex game was to have Nola so head over heels for you. I made a bad decision that could have ruined my relationship with my sister. I'd die without her. So again, I apologize."

The sincerity in her tone softened him a little bit, but he still didn't like her ass.

"I accept your apology," Hot Shot said as he stared straight ahead, navigating his car to his house. He looked forward to seeing Nola's face when she saw her sister. He intended on always keeping a smile on his wife's face. Twenty minutes later, Hot Shot pulled into the driveway, got out of the car, grabbed Lola's bags, and led her to the door. He opened the door and saw that Nola wasn't downstairs.

"Nola, come here, baby. I got something for you," he yelled so she could hear him.

Nola was walking down the stairs, focused on her phone, when she looked up and saw her twin sister staring at her with a huge smile on her face. She screamed and ran to Lola and gave her the tightest hug.

"Oh! My! God! I missed you so much, sister!"

"I've missed you more, sister," Lola said with tears streaming down her face.

Nola turned from her sister, smiled at her husband, and said, "Thank you, baby. Thank you so much!" She led Lola to the couch, and they began talking, so Hot Shot went up to the bedroom so the twins could have some privacy.

He still was amazed at how much they looked like each other. They were identical. The only way you could tell them apart was their different styles. They wore short pixie hairstyles that fit their small heads. Nola gave off a classier look, whereas Lola was more chic than Nola in how she wore her makeup, but one thing was certain: they were both gorgeous. Both had light brown eyes, smooth brown skin, slim waists, and an ass that could drive a man crazy.

Hot Shot was a lucky man, and he knew it. Nola made him happy, and now that everything was out, he felt there was nothing that could stop them from being happy for the rest of their lives. That thought made him smile. However, his smile faded as he got a text from JT telling him to give him a call. Immediately, he made the call and listened.

"We got a CI that is in with some Compton Pirus. They're beefing hard with the Mexicans in Compton and need some heavy artillery. So, I need you to meet with this CI and do what you do."

"When?"

"ASAP. I'll text you the number, and you take it from there."

"Understood. Is everything else still on point for tomorrow?"

"Yes, I got the director authorizing the weapons that will be here tomorrow. Once I put the chips inside them, I'll text you so you can come pick them up."

"Good. I'll get right on this assignment."

"Be safe, son."

"Always," Hot Shot said as he ended the call and waited for JT to send him the CI's number so he could call him and get the next assignment going. He felt good that he was doing something that could possibly save lives. Hot Shot took his job seriously.

The president of the United States had given him the green light to do what he had to do to do some good, even if he had to do some bad in order to do some good. He knew his family, especially his father, would be proud of what he did. That gave him solace, but his heart was cold toward Franco and the I-13s. They would pay. It will be his pleasure to see most of them in jail, but Franco had to die. If Hot Shot could find the actual killers who murdered his family, they would all die. But if not, at least he will feel his vengeance would be complete because he took out the head man who gave the order for his family to be slaughtered. Yes, Franco was as good as dead.

JT sent him the name and number of the CI. Hot Shot quickly dialed the confidential informant's number.

"Hello, This is Hot Shot."

"What's up, gee? I'm Piru Pete."

"When can we meet up?"

"Whenever you have time, gee."

"You in Compton?"

"Yep."

"Meet me at Tam's burger stand in thirty minutes. I'll be in a black Audi. We can go in and get something to eat and chop it up."

"Facts."

"Thirty minutes."

Hot Shot ended the call and quickly changed clothes so he could go do some good. Hopefully, he wouldn't have to do some bad first.

Chapter Ten

When Hot Shot entered the fast-food restaurant, he saw Piru Pete sitting at the back. Piru Pete was a small man with Blood tattoos all over his arms, neck, and hands. Hot Shot noticed how nervous he looked and wondered what his story was. He took a seat and waited for Piru Pete to speak.

"What's up, P?" asked Piru Pete.

"My name's Hot Shot."

"The P is how I speak, P. I feel you, though."

Hot Shot remembered that there is a distinction within the Bloods. You have Bloods, Pirus, Brims, Families, Bounty Hunters, and Swans. Most Bloods used the letter B in most of their speech, whereas Pirus used the letter P. So he understood what Piru Pete meant.

"What's good, Piru Pete? What you got for me?"

"The Pirus need weapons. The war with the Mexicans has gotten heavy out here in Bompton. The TTPs, FTPs, LPPs, HHPs, and the LHPs have put their differences aside to get at the Mexicans. That shows how serious this is because it's been some heavy beef within the Bompton Piru thang. The Rus have put their money together to get as many weapons as possible. I've been delegated to get the plug on the weapons. So, I need as many as I can get."

"Why were you chosen for this task?"

"Because I was known for my connections when I was heavy in the game. Nobody knew I got knocked when I was outta town, and the homies got at me to see if I had a plug on getting some heat. So to make my case disappear, this is where I'm at with it, P."

"I see. What are you looking for exactly?"

"Heavy shit, P. The bigger, the better."

"How much are they working with?"

"A little over 300 bands."

"I can get you whatever you need from AK-47s, AR-15s, to 9 mms."

"Do you have access to drums? The more shots, the better, P."

"Yes, I have AR-15s with two fifty-round drums and the same for the AKs."

"OK, that's bool, P. How much?"

"Fifteen hundred apiece for both the AR-15s and the AK-47s. It should be more with the drums, but this will make you really look good with your homies."

"Yeah, you're right, P. How much for the nines?"

"A thousand apiece."

"Can you handle 100 AKs and 100 ARs?"

"I can handle whatever you want."

"Bool. One hundred AKs and 100 ARs and twenty nines is 320 bands."

"Right. When will you be ready?"

"I got the money. I'm ready when you're ready, P."

"OK. Let me make the order, and I'll give you a call when we make it happen."

"That's what's up, P. JT told me everything would go smooth fucking with you, and that you will keep me protected."

"You won't have to worry about anything. Everything will be smooth."

"*That's* what's up, P."

Hot Shot stood, shook hands with Piru Pete, and said, "I'll get at you when I have the weapons, and we'll proceed from there."

"Solid," Piru Pete said and left the restaurant.

Hot Shot ordered a strawberry shake while he let Piru Pete leave. *Looks like there'll be a lot of Compton Pirus going to jail soon,* he thought with a smile. He was definitely about to do some good in the notorious city of Compton.

Nola and Lola were busy catching up while Hot Shot was gone. They were both so happy to be back together they couldn't stop the tears from flowing. Though they had different personalities, when it came to their love for each other, they were the same.

"When you switched with me to go do that time for me, I was at a loss for words, sister. I mean, I felt happy that you would do that for me. Yet, I felt guilty for letting you do that shit. But I knew there was no way I could ever have been put in a cell. I would have lost my mind."

Nola nodded her head in agreement and said, "I know. It's my fault you have claustrophobia, and there was no way I would ever let you go through that. There's nothing I won't do to protect you, sister."

Lola started crying again and said, "You gave up your child for me, you gave up your freedom for me, and what do my selfish ass do to repay you? Fuck your man. I hate myself for that, sister. I really do. I know you said you forgive me, but please know I am so sorry for that."

"You hurt me deeply with that one, sister. But I know how your freaky ass is. You just couldn't help yourself with your nasty ass."

"I tried, though, I really did. The more I tried to shake Hot Shot, the more he came at me. No excuses, though. I should never have done that to you. I'll forever be in your debt for your forgiveness, sister."

"Go on with that, Lola. You're my twin. You will never owe me. I do want you to apologize to Shot, though. He felt so bad about what you did. He felt as if he betrayed me, and that pain in his eyes when he told me that's how he finally figured out that you were playing like you were me hurt him deeply."

"That's the first thing I did as soon as I got into the car with him. I could tell he hated the sight of me because he looked at me. That's why I was shocked when he called me and told me that he was sending for me to spend time with you. He's a good man, sister, and you two deserve each other. I could tell he accepted my apology because those intense brown eyes of his softened just a little, and that made me feel good."

"Thank you for that, sister. I'm so glad you're here. We gotta go shopping. One thing about L.A. that I love is the top-of-the-line stores. Gurl, I cannot wait to get you in the Beverly Center. You'll be in heaven on earth when you see all the shit they got out there."

"Now, you know I can't wait for that." They both started laughing.

Cotton came into the house, saw the twins laughing, and said, "Oh shit, double trouble is in the house. What are you Dallas, Texas, girls laughing about?"

Lola looked at Cotton and wondered what his dick game was like.

Nola looked at her sister and shook her head because she could read the expression on her sister's face. "Where you been, Cotton, out on the prowl?"

"Nah, I had to go to the T-Mobile store to have them look at my phone, plus get me another screen protector. I keep dropping my phone and cracking up my screen. So, when did you get in town, Lola?"

"I got here a couple of hours ago. How do you like living on the West Coast?"

"Cool. How long are you going to be out here?"

"Depends on how much fun I'll have. You got something fun to do, chocolate?"

Cotton smiled his pearly white teeth and said, "Oh, I'm sure I can find something fun for us to do."

"I'm sure you can, baby," Lola flirted.

"Oh God, why don't y'all just go to his room and fuck him now to get it out of the way," Nola said, laughing.

"Gurl, I don't know why you're laughing. That sounds like a damn good idea."

"For real," Cotton said, staring at Lola as if he wanted to eat her up.

"Well, I was just playing, so save those freaky-ass thoughts. We still got more catching up to do. Cotton ain't going nowhere."

"You bet not, honey. I'm trying to taste you, so don't you disappoint Lola."

Cotton laughed and said, "Don't you worry 'bout a thang. That's one thing I won't do." He went into his bedroom, still laughing.

After Cotton closed the door to his bedroom, Nola asked her sister, "Are you serious, Lola? Since when have you been interested in Cotton?"

"I've always wondered what he was working with. Shit, since we're under the same roof, I might as well satisfy my curiosity. In-house dick saves me from going out looking for some Cali dick."

Shaking her head, Nola smiled at her sister and said, "You're truly special. I don't know what I'm going to do with your crazy ass."

"You know how I do, sister. Anyway, I need a shower, and then I want to go shopping."

"Now, *that's* what I'm talking about." Nola led her sister to the guest room and got her situated, then went into her room so she could get dressed.

***

Hot Shot came into the house and went straight upstairs. He entered the bedroom just as Nola came out of the bathroom with a towel wrapped around her. He smiled and said, "Mmm, looking so good I could eat you up, lady."

Nola let the towel fall to the floor, stepped to the bed, and said, "Come back with those words, Shot. You need a reward for bringing my sister to me," she said as she got on the bed and spread her legs and finger waved for him to come to her. So he did, and they made love passionately for thirty minutes.

Panting, Hot Shot said, "If I knew the reward for sending for Lola, I would've had her here on your first day home." They started laughing.

Chapter Eleven

JT called Hot Shot and told him he was ready for him to pick up the weapons for the Mexicans. Hot Shot assured him that everything had gone well with Piru Pete and gave him Piru Pete's order. Then he called Toker to let him know he was ready and for him to make the call to Franco. Toker was hyped and said, "Are we meeting up today?"

"Yes, I'm on my way to get everything together. I'll text you when I'm ready and give you instructions on where to meet my guy. Same as the last time. When my guy tells me he has the money, I'll bring everything. He'll tell you where to have Franco's men meet me."

"Franco will be with his people on this. He can't take any chances this time because that loss really hurt his pockets, so he wants to be hands-on with this shit."

"OK. Let him know what I said."

"Got it," Toker said and ended the call.

Hot Shot got dressed and told Nola that he was about to get the weapons from JT so he could handle the business with the Mexicans.

"Do you need me, baby?"

"It's all good. Cotton and I can handle it. So you go on and have fun with Lola. I'll text you when everything is all good."

"I think I should go with you, Shot. I don't need you going haywire dealing with those Mexicans."

"Don't worry, baby. All will be well." Before she could say a word, he gave her a quick kiss and left the room with her shaking her head.

Hot Shot checked the time on his phone after JT loaded the last of the guns in the backseat of Hot Shot's SUV. He texted Cotton.

Need you to meet me at the house in 30 minutes. It's time to get with Toker.

A minute later, Cotton responded to his text. I'll be there, Boss man.

Hot Shot went back inside of JT's house and saw his old army sergeant sitting at his desk, breathing heavily.

"You OK, JT?"

"I'm fine, son, just a little winded."

"When was the last time you had a physical? You are still smoking those nasty cigars, and God only knows when the last time you worked out."

"That's true. I do need to get back to working out, son. I'm fine, though."

With a serious expression, Hot Shot said, "I'm serious about that physical, JT. With this pandemic and COVID all around us, I think you should get a full physical, blood work and all."

"I'll get on it, son. Now, you go do what you do best."

Not wanting to push JT further, Hot Shot decided to let it go . . . for now.

"I'm on it. I'll check in with you after everything is everything."

They shook hands, and Hot Shot went to do what he did best but still wondered if his wife was right. Would he be able to control himself around Franco and not go haywire again? He was still trying to figure out how he would end Franco's existence. His patience was running out, and his thirst for revenge grew stronger daily.

***

"Sister, that Cotton is straight packing. I know every-thing is big in Texas but *damn*." Lola was laughing so hard that tears were falling fast.

"You're crazy. I can't believe you actually gave Cotton some. Now, he will be walking around here with his chest stuck out. He already thinks he's some super Mack Daddy. He'll be worse now."

"He has all the right in the world to think he's all that because, trust me, sister, he *is* all that."

"Ugh. Anyway, what do you want to do today? I thought we could get something to eat, then get a mani and a pedi."

"I'm with that. But look, I know you told me it's good that you're out of that jail, and Lord knows that I'm glad you're home, but why won't you tell me how in the hell you got out three years earlier than you were supposed to?"

Nola knew her sister would ask her that question sooner or later, and she hadn't yet come up with a believ-able story to tell her. So she would avoid answering her sister for as long as she could.

"Lola, I'm home, and it's all good. Get dressed so we can have a good day. I'm hungry, so hurry your ass up."

Lola started to push it but chose not to. Her sister was hiding something from her, and that deeply bothered her. They never kept secrets from each other, and before she went back to Texas, her sister would tell her how the hell she got out of federal prison three years early.

Cotton came into the house just as Lola stood up to get dressed. "Hey, baby, don't you be running from me now that I done got that ass."

"Baby, Lola runs from no dick, no matter how big it is or how good a man works it."

"That's good to know, so it's on later?" Cotton asked, smiling at the smirk on Nola's face.

Nola shook her head as she went upstairs, leaving them to continue their discussion, grateful for Cotton being the distraction she needed to escape her sister's curious stare. As long as they were alive, Nola had never kept anything from her sister, and by not telling her how she got out, it hurt, but she just couldn't tell her. Her loyalty to her husband was more important to her than telling her sister what really happened. *Am I wrong?* was the question swirling around in her head as she took off her clothes so she could shower.

Hot Shot pulled into the driveway and blew the horn. A minute later, Cotton came outside dressed in all black. He went to the driver's side of Hot Shot's SUV and waited for his instructions.

"We're about to go make this happen, so I need you to go to the parking lot of that Norm's restaurant on Imperial right off Crenshaw. Toker will meet you there. Once you know the money is on point, hit me, and then I tell you where I want you to tell Toker to tell his people where to meet me."

"Got it, Boss man," Cotton said as he turned and went to his truck to meet Toker.

Hot Shot waited a few minutes after Cotton drove off, then called Toker and told him where to meet Cotton.

"Once my man tells me the money is good, I'll tell you where to have Franco meet me."

"Facts," Toker said and ended the call. He turned to Franco and said, "I'm going to go meet Hot Shot's homie at the Norms on the South Side of Inglewood."

"The one on Crenshaw and Imperial?" asked Franco.

"Yes, Jefe."

"Then what?"

"After his homie makes sure the money's right, he'll get at Hot Shot, and then he will tell his man where to meet, and he will then tell me, and I'll hit you."

"All right, let's get this shit done."

As soon as Cotton counted the money, he called Hot Shot and told him everything was good.

"Great. Tell Toker to tell his people to meet at the parking lot of Morningside High School."

Cotton told Toker, and Toker called Franco.

"Morningside High School parking lot, Jefe."

Franco nodded as if Toker could see him and said, "This guy stays on the safe side of things. I like that. No one would look twice at us getting down in the open like that. Tell him I'll be there in fifteen minutes."

"Sí, Jefe," Toker said and ended the call. He relayed the information to Cotton.

Cotton called Hot Shot back. "They will be there in fifteen minutes, Boss man."

"Okay. I'm already here, and it's all good."

"Do you want me to pull up?"

"No, go back to the house. I'll handle this."

"You sure?"

"Yes."

"OK, be safe, Boss man."

"Always," Hot Shot said and ended the call. He quickly called Nola and asked, "Are you still at home, baby?"

"Yes, I just got dressed. Lola and I are about to go get something to eat, then off to the nail shop to get our nails and feet done."

"I need you to put that on pause, baby, and come to 105th Street and Yukon, right across the street from Morningside High School. I'm about to meet the Mexicans, and I will need you to follow them for me."

"Okay, baby. What do I tell my sister?"

"Tell her whatever you want. You can bring her with you if you want. I need to know where these Mexicans rest."

"I'm walking out of the house now," Nola said as she grabbed her keys, pistol, and purse. She quickly went downstairs. Lola was sitting on the sofa.

"Come on, Lola, we gotta take care of something real quick."

"I thought we were going to get something to eat. I'm hungry, sister," Lola complained.

"We'll eat, but first, I gotta handle something."

"Business?"

"Yes. Come on. We gotta move."

Lola put a pep in her step and followed her sister out of the house, curious to see what her twin had got going with that husband of hers.

Chapter Twelve

Franco's driver pulled a dark brown SUV right next to Hot Shot's vehicle, and Franco jumped out of the truck with two of his homeboys right behind him.

Hot Shot smiled as they approached him.

"You got everything I ordered, homes?" Franco asked as he reached his hand out toward Hot Shot.

"Indeed, I do. You can have your men check everything before loading them into your vehicle if you like."

"This isn't the setting to do all that, homes. I don't think you're the type of man that would play with his life by trying to play games with me," Franco said in a deadly tone.

"I don't play games. Period. I'm a businessman, and I expect those I choose to do business with to be as vertical as I am. Straight up and down all the way," Hot Shot responded in a no-nonsense tone.

Franco laughed and said, "OK, homie, let's get this shit loaded up. We got shit to get done." Franco's homeboys started transferring the boxes of weapons from Hot Shot's SUV to theirs while Franco and Hot Shot watched. Hot Shot checked the locator on his phone, saw that Nola was about ten minutes away, and knew he needed to stall for time. So he sent Nola a text.

Hurry. Running out of time.

She responded. Eight minutes away.

Make sure you park on 196th Street so you can follow the brown SUV.

Got it, baby.

He smiled because he knew she was speeding her ass off to get here. He loved his wife and how loyal she was. He thought about how sick he felt when he thought he had lost her. That was a feeling he never wanted to experience again. Then out of nowhere, Daun's face from Oklahoma City popped into his head, and he wondered why he was suddenly thinking about her. He felt a brief sadness creep over him as he remembered their brief love affair that ended abruptly with her being murdered senselessly. Life throws a lot at you. It's how you handle every trial and tribulation that defines you as a person. But still, a person feels when enough is enough.

Franco's homeboys finished loading the guns, and as they were getting back inside their SUV, Hot Shot received a text from Nola.

I'm here. I see you.

He texted her back. I need you to follow the brown SUV. Then once they reach their destination, I'll be right there.

Nola responded. OK.

Hot Shot sent one last text. Keep a distance between the SUV so you won't get spotted.

Nola responded with the fire face emoji that made Hot Shot smile. His wife was something else.

"Hope all is good. If you guys need anything else, get at me," Hot Shot said as he put his hand out to shake Franco's hand.

Franco shook hands with Hot Shot and said, "We'll get at you for sure, but this should hold us down for a while."

"I can also get my hands on anything else like drugs."

"Yeah? OK, I might check you out on that. Right now, let me deal with what I got." Franco turned, got into his truck, and they pulled out of the high school parking lot.

Hot Shot got into his vehicle and watched as Nola pulled from her parking space and followed the brown

SUV. She kept a nice distance behind Franco as he had asked her to. Then he grabbed his phone and called Cotton. When Cotton answered, he told him, "Meet me at the house. We got work to do tonight."

"I'm five minutes away," said Cotton.

"I'll be there in fifteen minutes," Hot Shot said and ended the call.

Nola and Lola kept their distance as they followed the Mexicans. It didn't take the Mexicans long to get to their location on the North Side of Inglewood. Nola passed the apartment building that the Mexicans pulled into, then turned the corner, parked, and called Hot Shot.

"We're on the corner of Hillcrest and Inglewood Avenue. The SUV pulled into an apartment building around the corner, baby."

"OK. I got your location on your locator. When you see Cotton and me pull by you, follow us so we can switch vehicles. I want you to take the Suburban, and we'll jump into the Audi."

"You sure you don't need me to stick around, Shot?"

"No. We're on a recon mission, baby. Nothing way out tonight."

"OK."

"Can you see the address on the apartment the Mexicans pulled into?"

"Yes, it's 11080."

"On Inglewood Avenue, right?"

"Yes."

"OK, see you in a few."

"Be careful, Shot."

"Always, baby. I'll be there in ten minutes," he said and ended the call.

"So, what's the get down on what we about to do?" asked Cotton.

"I was hoping we'd be able to follow Franco to where he rests his head and snatch him up. But they went into an apartment building, so that may be hard to do unless he remains in the brown SUV. But we'll play it however it goes."

"Is this Franco the one who did that to your family, Boss man?"

"He gave the order."

"That's just like pulling the fucking trigger."

"Exactly. Hopefully, I'll be able to get Toker to find out who actually murdered my family. If he doesn't, knowing I got the man who made the call will suffice."

"Fuck that. We gotta get all of them and do them dirty for real," Cotton said angrily.

"We'll see," Hot Shot said as he turned on Inglewood Avenue.

When he passed by Nola, she turned behind him, and he drove to the corner of Inglewood Avenue and Arbor Vitae and pulled into the parking lot of a grocery store.

No words were exchanged. Hot Shot and Cotton got out of the Suburban, and the twins got out of the Audi, and they switched vehicles. Hot Shot eased out of the parking lot and drove back to where Nola had parked. He had a good view of the apartment and silently applauded his wife for choosing the perfect parking spot so he could have the ideal angle to watch the apartment where Franco and his homeboys pulled into. They got comfortable because they didn't know how long they would be there.

Cotton pulled out his phone and began texting. Hot Shot grabbed his phone and called Toker.

"Tell me something, Toker. Do you know about an apartment on Inglewood Avenue, right off the corner of Hillcrest?"

"Yeah, my homie Tiger lives over there."

"So Franco doesn't stay there?"

"Nah, that's one of the spots where he keeps the drugs. So, that's where they took the guns, huh?"

"Seems like it. It's pretty risky to keep guns with drugs. That's automatic fed time."

"Facts. If Franco is keeping the guns there with the drugs, then he's only fucking with people he feels will never cross him. Tiger is his cousin and one of the homies he trusts most next to Puma and Termite."

"Do you know what Franco drives?"

"He has all types of whips, but mostly he's in a brown Tahoe."

"OK. Stay safe," Hot Shot said and ended the call.

"What you thinking, Boss man?" asked Cotton.

"If we're lucky, we can follow Franco when he leaves and find out where he lives."

"Then we can get at his ass?"

"Indeed."

"Good, I can't wait to tear into his punk ass."

"We wait and see if luck is on our side tonight. So, get comfortable. There's no telling how long we'll have to wait."

"I'm good. I'm having fun texting Yolanda and Lola. They are two of the freakiest broads I've ever met."

"Don't you have enough females on your line? Lola may turn out to be a headache. Thought you were feeling Yolanda?"

"I do feel her fine ass. But Lola is in-house pussy, and since I can't bring any of my broads to the house, I'm going to enjoy Lola's freaky ass as long as she's staying with us."

"You truly are incorrigible; you know that, Cotton?"

"I can't help it, Boss man. I'm addicted to sexy women."

They both started laughing . . . but they quickly stopped laughing when they saw the brown SUV pull out of the apartment complex. Hot Shot started his car as the vehicle passed them. He waited a full minute before he turned the corner and followed Franco's vehicle.

Looks like luck was on their side. Twenty minutes later, they watched as Franco's SUV pulled into the driveway of a house in the city of Lynwood. As Hot Shot drove past, he watched Franco get out of the truck and head toward the front door of the house. The driver of the SUV pulled out of the driveway and headed in the opposite direction, so Hot Shot made a U-turn and drove back past Franco's home.

Cotton smiled and said, "Looks like we got his ass, Boss man."

"Facts." Hot Shot wasn't smiling, though. Murder was on his mind, and he couldn't wait until he got his hands on the shot caller of the Inglewood 13s.

Chapter Thirteen

"Pull that big dick outta me and come on my face, you Black, nasty mothafucka," Lola screamed as Cotton did as she commanded. She rubbed all his semen over her face and licked her lips.

Cotton was so turned on by this dirty sexual act that he quickly put his dick back inside Lola's soaking wet pussy and began to fuck her harder than he had ever fucked a woman.

"Yes. Fuck me. Fuck. Me. Hard. Harder."

Cotton continued to pound away until he felt another orgasm mounting, and he couldn't resist coming inside Lola.

"I'm coming, baby! I'm coming!"

"Come on then, nigga, come in Lola's hot pussy." And that's precisely what he did. He came so hard he felt faint as he slid out of her pussy and fell back on the bed, trying to catch his breath.

"Damn, you gon' make me stay in Cali and forget about Texas, you keep dicking me like you just did."

"I thought you would make me move back to Dallas. That pussy is fire." They both started laughing as they cuddled up and drifted off to sleep, both totally sexually satisfied.

Meanwhile, Hot Shot couldn't sleep. All he was thinking about was how he was going to kill Franco. He didn't realize how he had been tossing and turning and woke Nola.

"What's wrong, baby? And don't you say nothing because you can't lie still for nothing. So talk to me, Shot."

"Ever since we followed that Mexican home the other night, I've been thinking of how to kill him. It's not going to be easy because I went to his house earlier and waited to see how he would move. His driver came and picked him up and took him back to that apartment on Inglewood Avenue. His home has security cameras all around, and it has the typical Los Angeles bar gate. So either I will have to follow him when he comes home and snatch him when his driver drops him off as he gets out of the car or get him in broad daylight as he's coming out of his house to get into the car. Either way is risky."

"Come on, baby, hold me, and let's get some sleep. We'll figure it out in the morning. I think with the three of us, we'll figure out something. Cotton and I got your back, baby, so don't stress on it. We'll get him; trust me," Nola said as she grabbed her husband and held him tightly. Soon, they fell peacefully asleep.

The following day after eating a big breakfast prepared by Nola and Lola, Hot Shot and Cotton sat in the living room talking about killing Franco. The twins entered the living room after cleaning up the kitchen.

Lola went and sat on Cotton's lap and said, "Hey, daddy, now that Lola has that belly full, you wanna go in the bedroom for a nice workout?"

"Can't right now, sexy. Time for business."

Hot Shot gave Nola a nod toward her sister, silently asking her to get Lola out of the room so they could talk. Nola shook her head no.

He sighed, then reached into a duffel bag he had next to his lap and pulled out two big stacks of one-hundred-dollar bills.

"Here's your pay for the last two moves we made with the guns. I'm waiting for this guy from Compton to get at me for another large order of weapons, so that'll be another ten thousand."

"Cool. How much is this, Boss man?" asked Cotton.

"Twenty bands."

Cotton smiled.

"Damn, Shot, you need to let me earn some bread like that," Lola said and laughed when her sister shot her a mean look.

"Mind your own business, Lola. For real, this is business time, not playtime. You can go in the other room if your ass can't be quiet," Nola said seriously.

"I apologize, but damn, can't your sister be a part of the team?"

"No. Now, be quiet."

Hot Shot wanted to smile but thought better of it.

"So, we're good until I get the call from the guy in Compton. The problem I want to toss around with you guys is Franco. We need to figure out a way to handle that with him. I've been to his house a few times, and the only way I can get him is to snatch him either when he leaves in the afternoon or when he returns in the evening. Both are risky. He has security cameras all around his house. I really don't care, but we gotta get this done."

"Why do you feel it will be risky to snatch him at his house, Boss man? I mean, we fuck the security cameras, and we'll be gooned up with masks and hoodies, so they won't see who we are. As for the cameras seeing what vehicle we're in, that won't matter because we'll be in a stolen ride, so it really ain't that difficult if you think about it."

"True," said Hot Shot.

"OK, but where will the actual deed go down? I mean, there has to be a place where you handle his ass, right?" asked Nola.

"We blow his fucking brains out in the car, then go switch up vehicles at a cool location with no cameras and get the fuck on," said Cotton.

"That looks like the only way we can move."

"So, when do we do this shit? It's way past time we get it over with," said Cotton.

"I'm going to check it out some more. I want to make sure everything is kosher before we move. We can't afford to slip because you know who will be mad as hell, and we can't let *that* happen at all."

"You got that right," said Nola.

"Yeah, I'm not trying to get checked like that ever again."

"OK, cool. Is there anything else we need to discuss?"

"Yeah, I got this dude I met, and he was asking me about some oxycodone and Percocet. I told him there ain't nothing I can't snatch."

"Where did you meet this guy?" asked Nola.

"His sister introduced me to him. She told me he's into getting serious paper and always looking for a new plug."

"If he's getting a large amount, then yes, we can get him what he needs. I'll make the call to make sure we have that on deck. Get at him and see how many he wants," Shot said as he stood, ending the meeting. He went upstairs and took a shower, still wondering if kidnapping Franco at his home would work. He didn't like having doubts about anything he was a part of, and for some reason, he didn't feel good about the decision. Maybe he was overthinking things. He knew he would go over it in his head many times before he would be comfortable handling Franco's kidnapping.

***

Back downstairs, Lola was on one again.

"Damn, sister, why won't you let me be on the team? You *know* I can help."

"This ain't Texas, Lola. The moves Hot Shot is making out here are on some different shit. You don't know anything about the get down out here in California," Nola explained.

"The streets are the streets no matter what state you're in, Nola."

"Explain to me what you will do to add to the hustle?"

Cotton raised his eyes but didn't say anything.

"Y'all take me to the club that pops the hardest, and I promise you, I'll have a few niggas who want to get down for whatever."

"We'll see. Friday, we'll go to the Melody Bar and see what you can do. I know Shot won't be with this unless you can show and prove."

"Sister, just take me to this Melody and watch how a Texas gurl gets down," Lola said confidently.

Cotton laughed.

Nola smiled and said, "We'll see, sister. Let me run it by my husband. We'll hit the Melody Bar Friday night if he gives me the go."

"Cool," said Lola.

"You still ready to give me that workout, baby, since the business has been handled?" asked Cotton.

Lola smiled and said, "You damn right. Let's go get at it, baby. The talk about getting money turns me the fuck on."

Nola shook her head as she headed to her bedroom and watched her sister go into Cotton's bedroom to be nasty. Damn freaks.

Chapter Fourteen

Nola woke up and saw Hot Shot standing by the bedroom window. She knew he was deep in thought on how to kill Franco. The revenge he needed was eating him up slowly, and she knew sooner or later it could go all bad. It was up to her to be his ride or die. She went to her husband and wrapped her arms around him. They stood gazing out at the early California sunshine.

"Come with me, Shot."

"Where?"

"I want to go to the beach and enjoy this morning before it gets too hot. So come on," she said as she quickly changed into shorts and a T-shirt.

As she led the way downstairs and they passed Cotton's bedroom, they heard moans and groans from inside. They looked at each other and shook their heads as they stepped outside and got into Hot Shot's car.

When they made it to the beach, they took off their shoes and walked out to the water. The ocean was cold, and they jumped as waves came close to splashing them. Then they strolled down the beach, gazing out at the cobalt-blue waters of the Pacific. This was what their life should be about . . . enjoying the simple things. All the money and the business of putting bad guys away could wait. Life was too short, and Nola would make sure they enjoyed however much time she and her husband had left on this earth.

"Shot, it's been a week since we decided how to deal with Franco. So what's got you on pause, baby?"

"Every time I go out to his place in Long Beach, I feel increasingly uncomfortable with taking him there. It just doesn't feel right, Nola. And as long as I feel like that, I refuse to make a move. I've ruled out the daytime. It has to be at night. But the thing about the night is his driver waits until Franco has gone inside his house. There's no shaded area where we can have the element of surprise on our side. And this isn't all about me, baby. Cotton's safety is my concern. I couldn't live with myself if something went left, and he got hurt. Every day I open my eyes, all I think about is blowing that Mexican into the afterlife. But I refuse to let my thirst for revenge put either of us in harm's way."

"I love how you truly care about Cotton. He's like your little brother, and together, there's nothing y'all can't handle. You've trained him, and he's no slouch. He can handle himself, baby. You need to have faith in that and get this done. It's time, Shot."

"I know, baby, I know," Hot Shot said as he stopped walking and faced his wife. "I'm going to let the next raid take place and see if that rattles Franco. Toker told me he's been stressed over the last raid. Not only did they lose the guns and drugs, but his pockets are also hurting from bailing out all his homies who could get bail. JT told me Inglewood Police would be raiding the apartment tomorrow morning. I want to see how spooked he'll be or if his moves will change. Then I'll get with him."

"Sounds like a plan, baby. I don't ever want you to go against your first mind, but this must be done so we can move on with our lives. You got plenty more good to do to be stuck in this rut behind that man. I've watched you move around in a daze, which ain't cool. I need you right mentally, or you might make a mistake, and we ain't having any of that shit, you hear me?"

"Say less," he answered as he pulled her into his arms and gave her a long kiss.

She pulled from his embrace and said, "Mmmm, let's get back home so you can make love to me. Cotton and Lola can't be the only ones in our house having some bomb sex." They both started laughing as they returned to the car.

When they were back inside their bedroom, their lovemaking was so passionate that neither realized how often they made each other reach their peak. Incredible orgasm after orgasm made them fall asleep in each other's arms, totally spent.

Hot Shot's phone rang and woke him. He saw that it was Piru Pete. When he answered the phone, Piru Pete told him that he had all the money and was ready to make it happen. Hot Shot told him he would call him back and promptly called JT.

"Have you got that other order ready? Piru Pete's getting on my nerves. We need to get this done."

"I was going to call you and tell you to come out to the house. I have everything ready to go. Also, we have another CI giving us some good intel on the Hoover Crips. I'll let you know everything when you get here, son."

"I'll be there within the hour."

"OK," JT said and ended the call.

Hot Shot saw that Nola was still sleeping, so he slid out of bed and went and took a shower. Then he dressed quietly, went downstairs, and saw Cotton sitting on the couch watching TV.

"I need you to stay ready. We've got a load to take care of in Compton later."

"OK, Boss man. Are you ready to deal with that Mexican? You ain't been yourself lately, Boss man, and I know it's because we ain't deaded that Mexican yet."

He smiled at Cotton and said, "Man, am I that transparent? You and Nola have me pegged. But don't trip. The time is coming. We'll talk later. I'm on my way to get the guns from JT. When I get back, I'll figure out how everything will go down."

"Say less," Cotton said as he returned his focus to the morning news.

When Hot Shot was pulling into JT's driveway, he saw JT having a coughing fit, and his heart gripped with worry for his boss. He got out of the SUV and stepped to JT with concern in his eyes.

JT waved his hand at Hot Shot and smiled. "Take that scared look off your face, son. I'm all right."

"No, you're not, JT. You need to see a doctor."

"Made an appointment already, son. This coughing is getting on my fucking nerves."

"It would help if you slowed down on those cigars."

JT gave Hot Shot the finger, and they laughed as they went inside the house.

"When will IPD make the next raid on the Inglewood 13s?" Hot Shot asked as he sat down.

"I haven't made the call yet. That's on my to-do list today," JT said as he sat at his desk and had another coughing fit.

Hot Shot had a worried look on his face when he asked, "I hope you're serious about going to the doctor tomorrow, JT. That cough sounds serious."

"It's tomorrow, son."

"OK."

"When are you going to get at Peter?"

"Later on today."

"OK, good. I have this CI that's a member of the Hoover Criminals."

"You mean Hoover Crips, right?"

"No. They don't consider themselves Crips any longer. They're Hoover Criminals now. So they flag under the orange bandanna instead of the blue one."

"Hmm, that's different."

"Right. I'll text you the info on this CI later. He's still being debriefed."

"What did he do to get caught up?"

"He got picked up at LAX with four kilos of cocaine. As soon as they got him, he started singing like a canary. And the information he gave was serious enough for me to get the call from the director. Your work is so valuable, son, that the higher-ups are impressed. What you've done with the Mexicans is really good. Now, the Bloods and the Hoovers . . . They will continue to be impressed. So let's keep at it, son."

"Say less," Hot Shot said.

"All of this snitching makes things easier on our end. It's funny because they telling inside the police car. Gotta love it."

"Facts. OK, let me get the truck loaded so I can move."

"I'll help you out in a sec. First, I gotta get at IPD and respond to the director. I'm swamped with emails."

"No worries. I got it," Hot Shot said as he stood up.

"Good. I didn't really feel like helping you out anyway," JT said, and they laughed.

"You funny. You make sure you let me know what the doc says. And don't you keep nothing from me, JT," Hot Shot said as he turned and went to load up his truck with the guns for Piru Pete. When he finished, he went back into the house and told JT everything was good, and he was on his way. JT waved him off and continued talking on the phone.

***

Cotton was lying on the couch when Hot Shot entered the house.

"What's wrong with you, Cotton?"

"When does Lola leave? That woman is a beast. I mean, I just broke her off for over an hour, and she still wants to get down. I'm tired as fuck, and on top of that, I've been neglecting my other cuties. Bitches blowing up my phone. The more females call me, the freakier Lola gets. It's like she's trying to fuck me so good that I won't get at my other hoes. The woman is a sex fiend."

"Thought that was what you liked."

"Don't get me wrong. I do love that shit, Boss man. But Lola is sucking me dry, and I love it. But I don't like in-house ass. Can't shake her ass because we live in the same house. Ugh."

Laughing, Hot Shot said, "You'll be all right, champ. I don't know how long she'll stay. I'll ask Nola for you."

"Did Nola tell you about us going out so Lola can showcase her skills on getting at new cats so we can serve them?"

"No, she didn't. What's up with that?"

"Lola wants to be with the business, and she told Nola that her game is tight enough to bring us some new clients."

"Please tell me Nola didn't tell Lola the business?"

"Nah, she didn't. After you dropped that bag on me, she told Nola she wanted to get in. So they gon' hit the Melody Bar or the Nile in Inglewood tonight so she can show Nola she still got it poppin'."

"Great. If she proves herself, then it looks like you'll be in trouble because she won't want to leave anytime soon."

"I know, and that would really be fucked up," Cotton said and slapped his forehead.

Hot Shot was laughing as he went upstairs. Cotton had finally met his match and realized he's not the top dog sexually when it comes to Lola. He knew firsthand how her sex game was back from when he had sex with her while thinking she was Nola. He was so embarrassed. He felt bad about Cotton's dilemma but couldn't do anything to help him, and that alone was funny. Too funny.

Chapter Fifteen

Hot Shot was on the phone with Piru Pete giving him instructions on how things would go down. Cotton was leaning against his truck, smoking a blunt that was so potent that Hot Shot felt as if he was getting a contact high. He stepped away from Cotton and continued talking to Piru Pete.

"This is how we'll rock with this, Pete. My man will meet you at the same place we met before. When he hits me and tells me the money is on point, I want you to meet me in Lynwood at the Plaza De Mexico in the back of the parking lot on the Food For Less side. Then we'll load you up."

"You sure that's cool? I mean, it's broad daylight. Won't that be dangerous?"

"I *know* you didn't just ask me that. Are you ready to proceed?"

"Yeah, P, I'm ready."

"My man will be at Tam's in twenty minutes."

"I'm ten minutes away, so it's all good."

"Cool," Hot Shot said and ended the call. He turned toward Cotton and told him that he wanted to follow him so he would take him to Tam's, where he was to meet Piru Pete. They got into their vehicles and headed toward Compton.

***

Hot Shot was parked across the street, watching Cotton's back as he met with Piru Pete. When he saw Cotton leaving the restaurant with a duffel bag in his hand, he started his SUV. He then got the text from Cotton telling him everything was kosher. He eased the SUV into traffic and headed toward Lynwood. Once he made it to the Plaza De Mexico, he parked at the rear of the parking lot and waited for Piru Pete. He didn't have to wait long. Piru Pete pulled into the parking lot and came and parked next to his SUV. He got out of his car and opened the back of his truck, and they silently loaded his vehicle with the guns. They finished in less than ten minutes.

"My homies will want more once they see I came through with this shit."

"No worries. Whenever they want more, just hit me, and we'll make it happen. You just make sure you're nowhere around these weapons because you *will* go to jail."

"I ain't trippin', P. None of these bitches will be near me after I drop them off."

"Say less," Hot Shot said, then got into his SUV and left.

When he made it home, he went upstairs and saw Nola getting dressed. He saw she had a cute little outfit she was about to wear lying on the bed. So he sat on the bed and stared at his beautiful wife.

"Why are you sitting there staring at me like that, Shot? You look like you wanna eat me up," Nola said, laughing.

"Maybe I do. But I see you got plans for the evening. When were you going to tell me about this Lola initiation to our business?"

"I didn't think I had to. It's harmless. If she gets some contacts, then it's all good. If she doesn't, she doesn't. No harm, no foul."

"What made you think of this? I mean, we don't need anyone in our business, baby. If you want Lola to stay longer, I don't have a problem with that."

"Lola was starting to ask me more and more questions about how I got out early and the business. So I thought this would back her up from me. She still sweats me daily about how I got out so fast."

"What have you told her?"

"To stop asking me questions and be happy that I'm home. But that tactic won't work much longer. Tonight's exercise will serve to keep her off my back. This is partly your fault, so don't be all salty with me."

"How is it partly my fault?"

"If you hadn't given Cotton his money in front of her, she wouldn't have gotten her nose open."

"Ahh, I see. Oh well, you and your sister have fun tonight and make sure your locator is on, so if you need me, I'll know where to come."

"My hero," she said, laughing as she continued to apply her makeup.

Meanwhile, Cotton and Lola were talking downstairs as he watched her get dressed. It was amazing how the two women looked exactly alike yet were totally different. Cotton was staring at Lola and wanted to grab her and fuck her silly she was looking so damn good

"You make sure you be careful and don't be *too* extra with it, baby. These Cali niggas move differently, and I don't want you getting caught up."

"Street niggas are the same in every state. They look different with their dress styles but move the same, and they all want that money. Trust, Lola knows what she's doing."

"I hear you but still, be careful how you get at these niggas. They different."

"Noted, honey. You just be ready to break Lola off real good after I return from the club."

"You got that, baby. I'll leave you to finish getting dressed. Be good."

"The last time I remember being good was in junior high school, sugar."

"Whatever, gurl."

Hot Shot was walking down the stairs just as Cotton came out of his bedroom. They went into the living room and took a seat on the couch.

"Everything went smooth, Boss man?"

"Yes, all is good. Did you get at your friend's brother?"

"He was out of town, but she told me she told him about me, and he's going to holla at me when he gets back in town."

"Good. We need to make as many moves as possible before we take the show back on the road."

"You ready to get outta Cali, huh?"

"The sooner, the better."

"You would think you'd want to stay here as long as possible with this being your home and all. But I know this shit with the Mexicans has you stressed, Boss man. I hate that shit. Let's do this fool and get it done."

"It has to feel right, bro. If it doesn't, I refuse to move. I'm not moving until I know for certain all will be good. I have to keep us both safe, Cotton."

Cotton heard the concern in Hot Shot's voice, which touched him deeply. "Boss man, there's nothing me and you can't handle together. Don't stress yourself by overthinking this shit. Let's get the job done, so you can have the closure you need, and we can get outta town and do what we do."

"I hear you. I got ten bands for you for the move we just made with Piru Pete."

"Now, *that's* something I like to hear. I love getting the bag for some easy shit like that. Does JT know what you're paying me for our get-down?"

"I'm in control of your pay . . . one of the perks of the job. All the money we make from doing what we do is mine to pay you, pay bills, and take care of us. Period. After what we've been through, I figure you deserve to get the bag. I got your back, bro."

"And you know I got yours, Boss man. What you got up for the rest of the night?"

"I'm waiting for Nola to bounce, then I'm going to chill out, have a drink, and watch Netflix for the rest of the night."

Shaking his head, Cotton said, "Nah, Boss man, I think we need to bounce to the club and watch the twins' backs. I got a funny feeling they may need us."

"They'll be OK. No need for us to be in the mix if they get into some shit. Nola will hit me, and we're not far from the club, so it won't take long to get there."

"I hear you, but you not feeling me. You've always told me to follow my first mind, and my first mind is telling me we need to go watch the twins' backs."

"You're right. I have told you to follow your first mind, so you go watch their backs, and I'll stay here and watch Netflix."

"You got jokes, huh? OK, that's exactly what I'm going to do. The Melody Bar usually is packed, so I'll keep an eye on them from a distance. If something pops off, I'll handle it."

"No need to get extra, bro. Stay low and watch their backs, that's all. I don't need you getting into any mess unless it's absolutely necessary."

"You know me. I'll blend right in and stay tucked."

"Yeah, I know you all right, so don't get caught up looking at the ladies in the club. Keep your eyes on Nola and Lola."

Cotton laughed and said, "If you know me that well, then you should know I know how to multitask."

Hot Shot laughed as he stood and went into the kitchen to see what he would make to eat. No stressing over Franco tonight. Just some rest and relaxation. Franco's life was on borrowed time, and when the time was right, he would get the pleasure of taking Franco's life.

Chapter Sixteen

Nola was dressed in a form-fitting sundress hugging her body, showing off her voluptuous curves . . . oozing sexy yet not revealing much. On the other hand, Lola wore a tight skirt with a sheer silk top exposing so much of her cleavage it almost looked as if she were topless. When the twins entered the Melody Bar, they felt the stares at them and couldn't help but smile, that knowing smile they shared. They were used to people staring at them because they were identical twins. Tonight, they knew the stares they were getting were from a bunch of lustful men drooling at how good they were looking. Even some women gave them the same type of stares, although a few wore frowns. They were also used to the hate from the females. They couldn't help it if their parents blessed them to be beautiful.

They stepped to the bar and ordered some drinks. Nola was happy to be out with her sister, so she intended to have some fun, get tipsy, and go back home and rock her husband's world. The thought of having Hot Shot inside of her was making her moist. She loved her some Hot Shot.

Once they had their drinks, they worked their way through the crowded club to the patio outside of the hot and sweaty club, where they found a table and took a seat as they bobbed their heads to the music and sipped their drinks. Lola's eyes were roaming, looking for the men with that gangster swag . . . the dope boy look that she knew very well. She spotted a few candidates but felt it was too early to make a move. She would work the room after she finished her drink. She was so happy to be with her sister here in sunny California and was determined to meet some men who would need her services so she could have a reason to stay. She didn't want to leave her sister. Though Nola told her she didn't have to rush back home to Texas, she still felt it would be better if she brought something to the table. That way, Hot Shot could see that she wasn't out there to be in the way. *Tonight's the night, and I'm going to make it pop off in my favor,* she said to herself as she sipped her drink.

Cotton was standing at the front of the club when Nola and Lola entered. He smiled as he watched as damn near every man in the front of the club stared at the twins. They were looking so damn good. He even saw a couple of dudes get pushed and slapped by their girls for staring so hard at Nola and Lola. That was funny. Once the twins headed to the back patio, he used that time to go to the bar, get himself a drink, and get at a few sexy ladies. Like he told Hot Shot, he definitely knew show to multitask.

Drink in hand, he eased to the back patio, found a discreet table, sat down, and watched Nola and Lola converse. He didn't have to wait long before he saw a man clad in a designer outfit with several expensive gold chains around his neck that screamed *dope boy*. This was going to be interesting, Cotton thought as he sipped his drink.

"Hello, ladies, my name is Fabian, and I must say, you two are the best-looking females in the club."

Lola took the lead and flirted quickly. "I must say, you're not looking bad with your handsome self."

"Thank you. What's your name?"

"I'm Lola, and her name is Nola."

Noticing Lola's Southern accent, Fabian said, "Where are you two from?"

"Dallas, Texas, honey."

"What brings y'all to sunny California?"

"I live here. My sister is out here visiting me," said Nola.

"Yes, but I'm looking for a reason to stay."

"Is that right?"

"Yep."

"Can I get you two another drink?"

"Sure," Lola answered for both of them.

"What y'all drinking?"

"Rémy Martin."

"Cool, I'll be right back," Fabian said as he turned and went to the bar.

"Not bad looking, huh, sister?"

"Yeah, he's cute. A little too much gold on, but he's good."

"That dark brown skin and that smooth bald head make him sexy, not cute. He's on his grown-man shit. And he is *definitely* in the game."

"Yeah, he has the look, but you never know. He might be an honest man who works."

"I doubt it, but we'll see," said Lola as she surveyed other men out on the patio of the club.

Before Fabian could return, another man approached the twins. He stood six foot six and sported some very long and neat dreads. He too had several gold chains on his neck, and Nola wondered if this was the look. Most of the men in the club seem to sport several gold chains.

They are getting their Mr. T on for real, Nola thought as she took the lead before Lola could start. She didn't want Fabian to come back and feel disrespected. That might start something.

"Hey, you, how are you doing this evening?"

"I'm good, baby. How about you?"

"I'm good. My name is Nola, and this is my sister, Lola."

"Pleased to meet you. My name is Skully."

"Hi, Skully."

"I assume you both know you're looking quite edible tonight."

"Edible? You saying you want to eat us up?" Nola asked, laughing.

"Facts."

"Mmm, that's different."

"No, for real. Y'all looking good."

"Thank you," they said in unison.

"Can I get you a drink?"

"We actually have someone bringing us drinks now."

"Cool. I'll get the next round for you."

"That's fine."

Before Skully could say anything, Fabian returned to their table with drinks in hand. He glanced at Skully, frowned, and gave him a dismissive look.

"Here you go, ladies. Two Rémy Martins on the rocks."

"Thank you, Fabian," Lola said as she took his hand in hers, so Skully could know it was OK for him to proceed with his conversation directed at Nola. "So, y'all don't do too much dancing in the club. I've only seen a few people out there getting their groove on."

Fabian laughed and said, "It's all about posting up, seeing who looks the best out here, baby."

"That's kinda lame, but I get it. In Dallas, niggas ain't too cool to get on the dance floor, and do they thang."

"It's not all about the floss, though. Come on, Nola. Let's get out there so you can show me how y'all get down in the South," Skully said as he held his hand toward Nola.

"Gurl, you better get out there and represent Texas," Lola laughed, and Nola frowned. But she stood and went out on the dance floor with Skully.

Fabian took Nola's seat and said, "So, you trying to let me show you the town?"

"I've seen pretty much everything, and to be honest, Cali is overrated. The beach is cool, and I had fun shopping, but other than that, it's just OK. But the weather is the shit, I will give you that."

"You ain't seen the town until you seen it with me, baby. There's much more than the ocean and shopping."

"Like what?"

"Give me your number, and let me come scoop you tomorrow, and I'll show you."

"I need to know more about you before I give up the digits, Fabian."

"What you wanna know?"

"Where's your woman? Don't lie, either. I respect the real."

"I don't have one woman who's all mine. I have friends, but I'm not with no relationship at this time of my life."

"I respect that. I don't want to be out with you, and some crazy bitch tries to get at me because it *will* be ugly."

"I feel you, but I don't do drama at all."

"What do you do to make your money? And remember, keep it a buck."

"I own a few car lots around the city. I also dabble in this and that."

"Mmm, I can dig it. I also dabble in this and that."

"Yeah? Shit, we may need to discuss this further, but not here, so give me your line, and we can have some fun and discuss some thangs."

"Give me your phone." He handed her his cell phone, and she punched in her number, then pushed the send button so she could have his. They were chatting it up, laughing, and having a good time until Lola saw her sister headed back toward their table with a frown on her face.

"Time to go, Lola, before I have to slap the shit outta that nigga, Skully," Nola said angrily.

"What happened?"

"We'll talk about it in the car. Let's go."

Skully came to their table and said, "I didn't mean to diss you. I thought you'd be with kicking it."

"When I kept moving your hand every time you touched my ass, didn't that give you a clue that I wasn't interested in your punk ass? Kick rocks, nigga."

"Bitch, you need to watch your mouth before you get the shit slapped outta your ass."

Skully just made a mistake because the one thing Nola and Lola hated most was being called a bitch. Lola was out of her chair in a flash.

"Who the fuck you calling a bitch, you bitch-ass nigga?"

Cotton saw the interaction with Lola, Nola, and some nigga with dreads and shook his head because he could see that the twins were angry. He eased closer so he could hear what was being said.

"I'm calling your sister a bitch."

"Come on with the disrespect, homie. If she's not feeling it, there's no need to get all bent out of shape," Fabian said, stepping between Nola and Skully.

"Nigga, who the fuck you think you are? Fuck you too, fool." Three of Skully's friends saw him having words with Fabian and strolled over to Skully's side.

"Oh, so now your boys here, you *really* tough, huh?" asked Lola.

"Come on, Lola, let's get the fuck away from these clown niggas," Nola said as she grabbed her purse.

"Clown niggas? Bitch, who do you think you are talking to?" asked one of Skully's friends.

Cotton quickly sent a text to Hot Shot. Get here as quick as you can. It's about to go down.

Hot Shot responded immediately. On my way.

Cotton quickly strolled over to where the commotion was, stepped between one of the men confronting Nola, and said, "Say, dog, let's back up off these ladies. They ain't trying to have any problems."

"Who the fuck are you, nigga? You better mind your own fucking business before you get fucked up," yelled Skully.

Shocked at Cotton's presence, Nola smiled. But her smile quickly faded when she realized that if Cotton was here, Hot Shot was on his way, and she wasn't trying to see her husband get stupid, so she tried to diffuse the issue before it got bad . . . real bad.

"Look, can't you guys just chill out and let us leave? There's no need for this shit to get ugly."

"Nah, fuck that shit. Fuck these ho-ass niggas," Lola said as she pointed her finger in Skully's face.

"Check it out. I'm not even tripping on the name-calling, dog, just trying to let this situation die down so we all can have a good time. No need for this wack shit, dog," Cotton said calmly.

Skully smirked and said, "Again, who the fuck is you, nigga? You better get the fuck because you don't want no smoke."

"Actually, dog, I *want* all the smoke. You and me can go to the back of the club and see what it do. Or do you have to have your boys help you out?" Cotton said with a look that showed no fear and that turned Lola on like crazy.

"Nah, he doesn't want no smoke, Cotton. You can see it in the bitch nigga's eyes. Fuck this shit. I'm with Nola. Let's go."

"Bitch, you got me fucked up, you and this bitch-ass nigga," screamed Skully. Cotton saw Hot Shot come to the patio, headed toward them, and smiled.

"I don't want to fuck you up, bitch nigga, so you need to back the fuck up, bitch-ass nigga."

Before Skully could respond, Hot Shot joined the small group, grabbed Nola by her arm, and said, "I don't know what's going on, but whatever it is, it's not for you, so let's go," he said calmly.

"OK, I see you bitches got some private security and shit. Say, nigga, you can get the fuck because we going to figure it out over here, nigga."

Cotton watched as Hot Shot clenched his fist and knew if Skully called Hot Shot one more nigga, it was about to get crazy in the club. And it was going to be all bad for Skully and his homeboys.

"Fuck these niggas, Hot Shot. They've been very disrespectful!" Lola screamed, pointing her finger inches from Skully's face. Skully slapped her hand and said, "You stepped in for you homeboy, huh? Fuck you and your homie nigga."

Hot Shot let go of Nola's arm, and in a blink of an eye, he was on Skully. Two quick blows to Skully's stomach knocked the wind out of him, added with blows to his mouth, nose, and jaw, and Skully was on the ground, knocked out cold.

"Damn," said Fabian.

"Whoa," said Nola.

"*That's* what your bitch ass gets, punk-ass niggas," screamed Lola.

Hot Shot turned toward Skully's friends just as one charged him. He was a bigger man, but Hot Shot knew how to fight him. There was no way that man could hit Hot Shot with his head down. Hot Shot stepped to the side quickly and hit the big man with two savage blows to the side of his head, and just like Hot Shot figured, the man fell on his face. The impact from the punches from

Hot Shot combined with his face hitting the ground, and he was sound asleep.

Skully's other two friends didn't want anything to do with Hot Shot. They quickly stepped to their friends and helped them to their feet. The security came, saw the two dazed men being helped by their friends, and shook his head.

"Is this over with?" asked the security guard.

"Yep," said Lola as she turned toward Fabian and said, "I'll hit you up tomorrow, boo."

"You do that, sexy. I got a feeling it will be a good vibe when we hook up."

"We'll see," Lola said as she followed Cotton, who led the way out of the club.

Once outside, Hot Shot and Cotton walked the twins to their car. Hot Shot sighed but didn't say a word. Nola knew that the silence, combined with the look on Hot Shot's face, told her he was pissed. Lola didn't understand that it would be best if she kept her mouth closed.

"I'm glad you came up here and fucked up those niggas, Hot Shot."

After the ladies were inside the car, Hot, Shot turned and walked away without saying a word to them. Cotton went to his car and laughed because he knew the twins were about to be in big trouble. That was extremely funny to him as he started his truck, sped out of the parking lot, and headed home so he wouldn't miss the show.

Chapter Seventeen

Hot Shot was furious and knew he should wait until he calmed down to speak to the twins. It would not be nice if he did otherwise, so he went to his bedroom and took off his clothes. By the time he had stripped, Nola had walked into the bedroom. He got under the covers and turned as if he was going to sleep. Nola preferred he was asleep. That way, she wouldn't have to hear his rant. She already knew what he was going to say. *"Why did y'all go out there starting stuff?"* Or *"What you were wearing was not suitable."* Yes, she was glad he was going to sleep. She went into the bathroom, showered, and went to bed, hoping it didn't get ugly in the morning.

The next morning after Hot Shot and Cotton finished their workout, Hot Shot called for Nola and Lola to come into the living room. Cotton had filled him in on what exactly happened, so he wasn't as mad as last night. However, he still needed to set things, especially with Lola. Her mouth was just too much. She was a firecracker of a woman, no doubt, but she would have to tone that stuff down while she was in his house. Nola and Lola came to the living room and sat on the couch.

"Last night, you two went to the club to see if Lola could meet some people to do business with us. I wasn't feeling that but said whatever. From what Cotton said, it all went left when the guy with the dreads got disrespectful to Nola. I feel that, and there isn't anything wrong with how you handled *that* situation. When I'm here or anywhere,

I like to handle myself in a low-key way. I don't want any extra attention. But that's me, and I can't expect that from you. But when I have to get out of my bed to get involved in extra stuff, I have a problem with that."

"Everything was Gucci when you got there. Cotton had checked the fool or was about to get with that nigga's ass."

Nola cringed because she knew what Hot Shot was about to say to her sister.

"That's another thing I feel the need to speak on. Lola, I don't care for the use of that N-word. I don't care to hear it around me, and for sure not when someone is talking to me. So I'm asking you respectfully, please, don't use that N-word. The way I was raised was always to respect four fellow Blacks. That word is a disgrace and a total disrespect to Black people. You may not agree with it, but please respect my wishes."

Cotton cringed, expecting something crazy from Lola.

"You know what, Hot Shot? You got that, and I apologize for the use of that word. Nola has told me how you don't like the use of it, so that's my bad. About last night, though, I was heated, and that clown had called us one too many bitches, and when that word is directed toward me or my sister, then, yeah, that's a problem, and that pretty much sums up the evening. The fool Skully got too close to my sister, and she checked his ass. He then thought to come and explain himself, and it went left from there."

"I understand that."

"On the business side, I got at Fabian last night when we got home. He deals with meth. I asked what he paid for a kilo, and he said he gets ten pounds at a time for $1,200 a pound. So I told him I'd check with my people and see if I could get him a better price, and he was excited about that. I'm going out with him this afternoon. I'll vet him more before I decide to get at you with the green light to fuck with him. He seems like he's about his business, but you never know. Especially out here because these Cali fools be faking it for real. I saw so many dudes wearing fake jewelry last night that it didn't make any sense."

"I know, girl. I almost asked a guy how much his chain was but thought better of it," Nola said, laughing.

"That's how these suckers rock, and it kills me because they be thinking they fly with all that fake shit on," said Cotton.

"Yes, that's crazy, but it is what it is. That sounds like it may just work with that Fabian cat. Keep me posted. Make sure you let him know there's nothing that we can't get. We trying to make all the money from any lane."

Proud of herself, Lola said, "No worries. I'm on it."

"All right then, that's all I wanted to say, so we're good. I'm about to get showered and make a few runs."

"Since Lola has plans for the afternoon, do you mind if I hang out with you, baby?" asked Nola.

"That's cool."

After Hot Shot and Nola left the room, Cotton told Lola that he needed to talk to her for a minute.

"What's up, boo?"

Cotton didn't want to sound like he was jealous, even though that's exactly what it was. "I'm not feeling you going out alone with that clown, Lola."

"It's business, boo—no need to be jealous. I got my Cali man. I don't need or want another."

"I'm no Cali man. This is and always will be Texas, baby."

"I know. I was just messing with you. Don't worry. Fabian ain't getting none of this cat. It's all yours, baby." She kissed him, and that made him feel better.

He still was irked that she was going out with Fabian, but what else could he do or say to stop her?

Nothing.

He went outside to smoke a Black & Mild and called Yolanda to see what was up. It had been a minute since he got at her. He got her voicemail and left a message. Looks like he was stuck with nothing to do for the afternoon, so he went back inside the house and turned on the TV.

Hot Shot took Nola to lunch at The Wood, a barbeque restaurant that he heard was pretty good. The food was good, a little pricey, but still good. After they left, he called JT to see how his doctor's appointment went.

"Talk to me, old man, and don't leave out anything."

"Well, son, looks like you may have to deal with me a few more decades. The doc says I'm in good shape and gave me something for the cough."

"That's good to hear."

"Yes, son, it was really good to hear. On another note, the Inglewood Police Department has been giving another tip on the Inglewood 13s. They're raiding them this evening."

"Good. I want to see how Franco reacts to this one."

"I also talked with a friend at the Compton Police Department, and they will follow the tip I gave them. I've been watching the monitors on the guns, and they have still been in the same place since they were purchased."

"Inglewood or Compton?"

"Both."

"Cool. I've made a few new contacts, one for some meth and the other for some pills."

"I do believe we can make that happen. Let me know when you're ready. I'm about to pick up my prescription and head on back home. You stay safe, son."

"Always," Hot Shot said as he ended the call.

"How is JT doing, baby?"

"He's good. He had a bad cough that bothered me. But he went to the doctor today and said all is good."

"That's great. Where are we going now?"

"I just want to bend a few corners and see what things look like around Inglewood. The Mexicans are about to get raided again, and I want to see how Franco reacts. Until then, I'll keep doing my recon on his ass."

"That's what this is, recon, huh?"

"Yep."

"You seem to be acting more like yourself lately, and I like that."

"Say less. I decided to just go with the flow. When the time is right to get at Franco, I'll know it. Until then, it's business as normal. Doing some bad to do some good."

"That's right, baby," Nola said as she grabbed his hand and gave it a little squeeze.

Chapter Eighteen

Hot Shot got the call from JT informing him about the two raids made by the Inglewood Police Department and the Compton Police Department. Both went well, with a combined number of forty-six arrested. Hot Shot smiled at the news. More assholes off the streets.

"The director told me to tell you 'good job' and 'continue the good work.' I could tell he was excited. He couldn't wait to get off the phone, so he could tell the president what an outstanding job you're doing."

"That's cool. Now, I want to see how fast the Mexicans and the Pirus get back at me. Did you check on the meth and Percocet?"

"Yes. Tell me when you need them, and I'll have them for you. These will take a little time to get the sensors inside the packages, so make sure you buy me some time."

"No worries. All is good. I think I'll take the team out to dinner to celebrate."

"That sounds like a good idea. Enjoy yourselves. I'm proud of you, son. Keep at it and stay safe."

"Always," Hot Shot said and ended the call. Then he called Cotton to see what his plans were for the evening.

"What's good, Boss man?"

"Do you wanna take the ladies out to eat tonight?"

"That's cool. I ain't doing shit. I just got at Yolanda's brother, and he wants to get two thousand pills. Oxy and Percocets."

"OK, let him know you'll get with him when you get lined up. I'll get at JT and make the order."

"Cool. I told him four dollars a pill since he said he got them for six dollars each, and he'll get at least a thousand or more."

"Good job. Let me get at JT and check on the twins and see what they want to eat tonight."

"All right. I'll be back at the house in an hour or so."

"Say less." Hot Shot ended the conversation and called JT to inform him about the order of Percocet and oxyco-done. After he ended that call, he called Toker to see what he had to say about the raid.

"What's good, Toker?"

"I was just about to hit you up. They hit hard this morning, and Franco is stupid pissed off. He knows someone is snitching and is on the verge of killing everybody. I'm good because he knows I didn't know where the guns were. He wants to meet at our park for a meeting later. What really has him pissed is Termite, Puma, and four other homeboys were caught in the raid, and he had just bailed them out, so they stuck."

"Oh, well, the life of a gangster is a hard one."

"Facts. It's hard for me not to laugh because he is so hot, he's talking superfast in Spanish, and he sounds straight crazy."

"You make sure you don't do anything that can put you in harm's way, Toker. I mean that."

"I'm good. OK, let me go. I'll hit you later to let you know what went down at the meeting."

"Say less." Hot Shot ended the call and went downstairs to see the twins sitting on the couch talking. Both looked casually sexy in matching maxi dresses. He shook his head because it was still strange to see them together, knowing that he had made love to both. He quickly dismissed that thought from his head.

"Hey, baby, what are you doing today?" asked Nola.

"Nothing much. Might go get the cars washed and run a few errands."

"I got with old boy, and he wants to get a couple of pounds of meth to try it out. If it's Gucci, then he's ready to get more," Lola said.

"OK, I'll make that call and let you know when I'm ready. If this works out, you can make you a nice piece of change."

"Now, you *know* I like the sound of that. Fabian is cool but kinda corny. I think he's serious about his paper, though."

"*That's* what's up. How do y'all feel about going out to dinner with me and Cotton this evening?"

"I'm with that," said Nola.

"Me too. Where are we going?" asked Lola.

"I don't know. What do y'all wanna eat?"

They sat there in thought, then Nola said it didn't matter to her. "Can we go somewhere out on the beach?"

"Yeah, we can do that. We can go out to Malibu and eat at Mastro's if y'all in the mood for a good steak."

"We from Texas. We *always* down for a steak as long as it's good," said Lola.

"That's what's up then. I already got at Cotton, so I'll make the reservation and let y'all know when we'll leave."

"OK, baby," Nola said and kissed him.

"Where's my black stud at?"

"He had to make a run. He said he'll be back in an hour," Hot Shot said as he left the house feeling good. Today was a good day in more ways than one, and he hoped for more days like this.

"So that's how you gonna do me, Cotton? Just up and leave all fast? I told you I took the day off. I thought we

could spend the day together. We don't do shit anymore,"
Yolanda said, pouting.

"It's not like that, baby, but I got a lot on my plate today.
And for real, I forgot you said you had the day off. I don't
ever want you to be salty at me, baby." He went into his
pockets, pulled out a large wad of cash, peeled off ten one
hundred-dollar bills, and gave them to her. "Go have a
spa day on me, baby. Get your hair and nails done and
have a good day, and I'll make it up to you, all right?"

She smiled and gave him a tight hug and a kiss. "You
are so damn good to me, baby."

"Say less. Now, let me go and make sure you send me a
picture of you looking all sexy. And make damn sure you
have a female give you that massage. I don't want no man
touching on my baby phat ass."

"You silly, but I'll make sure it's a female, baby." She
gave him another kiss, and he left. He really liked
Yolanda, and she was definitely going to be around for a
while. But Lola staying with them made it hard for him
to move around like he wanted. She knew the business,
but she didn't know their business, and with her being so
close, he felt it would only be a matter of time before she
figured things out. He made sure he stayed on his toes
because she always had questions about the business.
He had to keep her in left field because if she found out
what they were really doing, he didn't think she would
take it as well as Nola did. After all, Hot Shot was why her
brother and cousins were in federal prison.

Oh well, he thought as he got in his truck and pulled
away from Yolanda's house. Turning on Long Beach
Boulevard, he noticed a blue Ford turn behind him. He
couldn't tell who the driver was, but he felt they were
following him. He turned on Carson Street, headed
toward Compton, and the blue Ford continued to follow.
When he got to Del Amo, he made a left, then a right on

the 710 Freeway. When he got on the freeway, he put the pedal to the metal and watched his rearview to see how far he had left the people following him. They tried to speed up, but his powerful truck was too much for them. He took the 91 West to the 110 North, got off the freeway, then got back on the 110, this time headed south toward San Pedro. He relaxed because he knew for sure he had lost his tail. Then he called Yolanda and asked her if her baby father had a blue Ford.

"Yeah, it's his mom's car. Why?"

"It looks like he hasn't learned his lesson. Call him on the three-way for me, baby." Cotton was boiling as he waited for Yolanda to click back over with her baby father on the line.

"Cotton, you there?"

"Yeah, I'm here, baby. Check this out, bro. If you *really* want problems, you can get them. I thought you had it figured out the last time. If you want more, then you can definitely get it."

"Fuck you, cuh. Yeah, I want to run that fade back, cuh."

"Whenever you want it, you can get it. Trying to follow me in a four-cylinder isn't a smart idea, chump. Especially when you're trying to follow me incognito, you dumb-ass clown."

"Yeah, whatever, cuh."

"Doug, I'm calling your mother and telling her the stupid shit you doing in her car."

Laughing, Cotton said, "Yeah, that's right, baby. Tell his mama on his childish ass. I'm out. Enjoy the day, baby. See you when I see you, Doug." Cotton set his phone down and sighed with relief. *These L.A. gang-bangers are a fucking trip,* he thought as he headed home.

Chapter Nineteen

Hot Shot was lying in bed listening to Nola lightly snoring, and he couldn't help but smile. They returned from dinner and went straight to the bedroom where they made love for a few hours nonstop. They came so many times that neither had any energy left. *If taking her out to the beach for a nice steak dinner brings about a sweet dessert like that, then we should do it more often,* Hot Shot thought as he continued to stare at his gorgeous wife. He was happy for the first time in his life. He was truly happy.

After his parents were murdered, he thought he'd never find happiness. His wife's love overrode the hatred he had deep in his heart for Franco. Love was truly powerful. Even though he's been able not to let his hatred consume him, Franco still has to die. He had to kill the man that ordered the murder of his parents. His days were numbered. But for now, he'd continue being patient and wait until the time was right for him to strike.

Cotton couldn't believe the stamina Lola possessed. That woman seemed to never run out of energy. It was like the longer they made love, the more she wanted. She had to have at least four orgasms for his two. He was staring at her smooth legs and pretty, light brown skin. She was definitely a dime. If he wasn't against loving a woman, he could see himself loving Lola. He

couldn't deny that he was feeling for her in a way he
never expected he would. It was time to talk to Hot Shot
about starting Lola's exit plan. He couldn't afford to let
love interrupt his life. He never could love again. Love
hurts. But sex was good, especially with this fine woman
lying next to him naked.

He rubbed her smooth legs and felt himself start to
get hard. He moaned as he dipped his head, put one of
Lola's nipples into his mouth, and sucked it lightly until
she moaned and stirred. Finally, she opened her eyes and
smiled at him as she pulled him on top of her. She spread
her legs, and he eased his dick inside of her, and it was
on again. They made love until it was time for Cotton to
get up and do his daily workout with Hot Shot. When
he finished, he returned to the bedroom and saw Lola
was still asleep. He was not about to wake her because
he was dead tired. He barely made it through Hot Shot's
rigorous workout.

He jumped into the shower and let the hot water
soothe his aching body. After he finished, he was ready
to start his day. He dressed quickly and quietly. Then he
went to the living room to watch TV. He was happy that
Hot Shot seemed to be himself again. He didn't know
what had happened to him, but he was glad his friend
acted like his old self. He knew how much Hot Shot
wanted to murder that Mexican, and in time, he would
get him. Cotton did not doubt that. But now, it was time
for business.

Cotton was about to meet up with Hakeem, Yolanda's
brother, so that he could buy some pills. Hot Shot had
given him the package for Hakeem last night, so it was
time to do some bad to do some good. He loved this situation . . . being able to sell drugs and not have to worry
about going to jail is the shit. He had a pass to make
money illegally and help get fools off the street at the

same time. He never thought he would be a crime fighter of sorts, and it felt good to know he was doing something right for the first time in his life.

Yeah, life was good right now. So he grabbed his phone and texted Yolanda's brother to see if he was ready to move.

"What up, gee? You ready to get it in?" asked Cotton.

"Yeah, I'm Gucci, bro. Where you want to hook up at?" Hakeem asked.

"We can meet at your sister's house. I can be there in twenty minutes."

"OK, bro, that's cool. See you in twenty."

"Bet," Cotton said and ended the call. He was about ten minutes late getting to Yolanda's house, but it didn't matter because Hakeem wasn't there when he pulled up. He had his pistol on his lap just in case Yolanda's son's father arrived, trying to get his head split. Cotton was hoping he wouldn't have to hurt the man. He shrugged it off and waited for Hakeem to pull up. He was about to call Hakeem just as he pulled in front of him, got out of the car, and came to his truck.

"What's good, bro?" Hakeem said after he climbed inside Cotton's truck.

"It's all good, dog. Just another day on the grind," Cotton replied as he gave Hakeem the two packages of pills.

"That's what's up." Hakeem passed the cash to Cotton and was looking at the pills. "I'll be getting back at you by the weekend. These joints are going fast. As long as you can stay on deck, you'll see me twice a week."

"Hit me up a day ahead of the time, so that way, I'll be ready when you need me."

"Say less." Hakeem shook hands with Cotton and got out of the truck. Cotton watched as he got into his car. Then he started his vehicle and headed back home.

When he arrived, Hot Shot and the twins were sitting in the living room. He tossed the stacks of one-hundred-dollar bills to Hot Shot and told him everything with Hakeem went smoothly.

"That's the business right there. You should have let me ride with you."

"Nah, I handled that shit, Boss man. Hakeem told me that if the pills are on point, he'll holla at me at least twice a week. So I told him to get at me the day before he needed me. That way, I'll have time to get at you to get me good."

"That's cool. I'll make sure we'll be ready for him. What you got up for the rest of the day?"

"Not much going on right now. I'm about to go lay it down for a minute. I'm seriously tired." Cotton cut his eyes toward Lola and told Nola, "Please take your sister shopping—the nail shop—anywhere because I don't have the strength to mess with her."

"You know damn well you are wrong for that, Cotton. I was asleep, and your horny ass started it this morning. Now, you are talking that mess. Boy, bye," Lola said, laughing.

"Sorry, Cotton, I don't have any plans for us today, so you're out of luck, buddy. Looks like you have started something you cannot handle," Nola said, laughing.

"Whatever."

"Lola, any word on when your man Fabian wants to get down?" asked Hot Shot.

"He told me he would be ready whenever I'm ready. So I was waiting on you to get at me."

"I got that for you, so you can make the call and handle that today."

"OK, let me do that right now," Lola said as she made the call.

"Looks like everything is going smooth, baby."

"Say less. It's all good."

Lola ended the call with Fabian and told Hot Shot that she would meet Fabian for lunch and handle the business then.

"That's cool. I got three pounds of meth in the closet. Grab it when you're ready to move. I'm about to go bend some corners. I'll get back at y'all later."

"Where are you going, baby?" asked Nola.

"I need to get with Toker and see what's up with him."

"OK. Do you want me to make lunch or go on and cook dinner?"

"Dinner's fine."

"Anything specific you want to eat?"

"Whatever you make is good with me, baby. I love your food."

"Facts. You be careful out there, baby."

"Always. OK, let me bounce."

"Come on, Cotton, let's see if your ass is as sleepy as you claim."

"Lola, I'm not messing with your ass."

Laughing, Lola replied, "Whatever you say, baby."

Smiling, Cotton shook his head as he followed her into the bedroom. Then Nola kissed Hot Shot and went into the kitchen as Hot Shot left to meet with Toker.

Everything was well with the team. Now, all he needed to do was murder Franco. That thought took the smile off his face. "Yes, it's about time I get with Franco," Hot Shot said to himself as he got into his car. *Time's up, Franco.*

Chapter Twenty

Hot Shot met Toker at a soul food restaurant called the Soul Food Shack in South Central L.A. because he didn't want to meet in Inglewood. Franco was so shook that Toker wouldn't be surprised if Franco had him followed. Hot Shot got into Toker's car, and he could tell something was wrong. So he would let Toker speak first and see where this conversation would go.

"Homes, the neighborhood is so hot it makes no sense. Franco is on the warpath and swears that when he finds out who is snitching, he will kill their entire family. Only three people knew where the guns were kept; they were his family members, so he's looking at everybody now. He wants me to get at you with an order of guns but only half what he previously got. The money is fucked up now from bail money to lawyers."

"When does he want the weapons?"

"ASAP. He told me the sooner, the better."

"OK, I'll make the call and get back at you this evening. Are you good?"

"Yeah, I'm straight. He knows I didn't know where the guns were kept, so I'm good. I hope he keeps it that way. As long as I don't know where they are, I'll be good."

"OK. If you even think for a minute you're in danger, hit me, and we'll get you away somewhere safe."

"I won't front, though. I'm a little spooked, but I know I'm good. Franco's putting everyone under the microscope to see if he can get an idea who's doing the snitching."

"I feel you, but you're good, and this will end soon."

"When?"

"Soon," Hot Shot said and got out of Toker's car, ending the meeting. As he drove home, he realized that it was time to bring this mission to an end . . . which meant it was time for Franco to die. He walked into the house and was bombarded with questions from Lola and Cotton.

"Where have you been, Boss man?"

"I hit you several times. I need some more meth for Fabian. He's waiting on me to get back at him. Can you make the call for more meth?"

"Yeah, I need more pills too. Yolanda's brother is ready for more."

"Will you two relax? You know how the get-down is. I have to make the call and see when I'll be able to get everything."

"Right, so when you're gon' make the call?" asked Lola.

"That part," added Cotton.

"I'll take care of it now and let you two know when everything will be everything," he said as he pulled out his phone and called JT. When JT answered, he checked with Cotton and Lola to see what they wanted, then relayed their orders to JT.

"I need a couple of days to make sure we have what you need, son. I'm sure we have it, but it's going to take me a day to get things right. It's a tad tedious bugging those pills and packages of meth. I got what I needed, though. I know where the meth is being held as well as the pills. I intend to get right at the LAPD and the Long Beach Police Department for these next two packages. Hit 'em quick and hard, and they'll be out of the way."

"OK, that's cool. I also need another order of weapons, half of the order like we got the last two."

"Wow. Those Mexicans are playing with some serious money, I see."

"Yes, but their resources are running low."

"Might be time to bring this to a close, huh?"

"Definitely."

"OK, I'll get on everything for you."

"Great," Hot Shot said and ended the call.

"Are we good?" asked Cotton.

"Yes, everything will be ready in a day or so. You know the routine. I want both of you to be careful with who you're dealing with. I know y'all said it was cool, and you've already got at them once, so it's all good. But out here, things can go left real fast, so make sure you're always on point. For real, Lola, I'd prefer that Cotton goes with you when you get at Fabian again."

"I hear you, Shot, but I'm good. No worries about Fabian, though. He wants this pussy bad."

"I disagree with you, Lola. You don't really know this dude. So, do me a favor, please, and when you get with Fabian, take Cotton with you . . . even if he has to watch your six from a distance."

"I don't have a problem with that. Cotton can trail me and watch me handle the business."

"Thank you. All is good then?"

"Yep," said Cotton.

"Indeed," said Lola.

"Good. Where's Nola?"

"She went to the grocery store to get a few things for dinner."

"That's cool." Then suddenly, Hot Shot's phone rang, and he smiled when he saw that it was Piru Pete's number.

"What's good, Piru Pete?"

"It's all good for us and all bad for the homies. After the raid the other day, niggas is mad as fuck out here in Bompton."

"Do me a favor and try not to use that N-word. It disturbs me at the highest level," Hot Shot said in a serious tone.

"My bad, P. Anyway, some of the Rus who playing with some serious money got at me and wanted to see if I could get them some more straps from you."

"What do they want?"

"Ten AK-47s and ten AR-15s with the fifty-round drums."

"OK. Let me make the order, and I'll hit you when they're on deck. Tell them that's twenty bands."

"Bool. They with that."

"All right. I'll get at you in a day or so."

"That's right," Piru Pete said and hung up the phone.

"Looks like things are popping on our side. Y'all keep handling things, and we will keep winning."

"So, that means I'm a part of the team?" asked Lola.

"I guess so," Hot Shot said and smiled, knowing that his answer irked Cotton to the highest level.

"That part," Lola said happily.

"All right, I'm going to get me some rest. I'll get at you two later."

Cotton waited until Hot Shot went upstairs and then smiled at Lola.

"You're smiling at me like that because . . .?"

"You already know why I'm smiling, girl. Get your ass in that there room and get naked. It's time for me to put this dick deep inside that wet pussy."

Lola laughed but said nothing. Instead, she turned around and followed Cotton's order. They went into the bedroom and started having some great sex. Cotton didn't want Lola staying too long—at least that's what he was trying to make himself believe because he wondered how he would feel once she took her supertight pussy away from him. He was smiling because he knew what he wanted, and honestly, he didn't want Lola to leave. He wasn't in love with her. He was in love with the way they had sex. It was the bomb.

Chapter Twenty-one

Franco was pacing back and forth, staring at his home-boys, wondering which one was snitching. For the life of him, he didn't have a clue who was betraying him. And not only were they betraying him, but they were also betraying their gang and the codes they'd sworn to live by. This was unacceptable. Over fifty I-13s were in the park, standing silently in front of their leader, and each one was beyond nervous. Not one of them was beyond being disciplined, and they knew that when Franco was on the warpath, any of them could get it.

"I can't figure this shit out. One loss like that I get because shit like that happens. But two losses so heavy, back-to-back, is fucking crazy. We have a rat among us, and I want you to know, whoever you are, I'm going to find out, and I'm not only going to kill you, but I'm also going to make you watch as I murder your closest family members for your act of betrayal to our gang," he vowed.

Even though Toker knew his cover was secure, he was still scared shitless. He had to keep telling himself that he was good, and there was no way Franco would find out he was the reason why they'd gotten hit by the police for all those guns. Toker didn't know how to play poker, but he absolutely knew he had to keep his poker face on because he didn't want to show any signs of fear to make Franco think he was the snitch in the gang.

"Toker."
"Jefe."

"Did you get at that fool about more guns?"

"Sí, Jefe. He said to give him a day or so, and he'll be ready."

"OK. At least we'll be able to get some more guns. We cannot go this long without weapons. We'll be weakened if we don't have guns, and that just can't be. So if anyone knows anything or has a clue about who this rat is, you better get at me as soon as you find out or even *think* of anything, or I'll look at *you* as the rat, and you *will* reach the same fate, am I understood?"

In unison, every I-13 in the park said, "Sí, Jefe."

"I have a question, Jefe," Tiny, a short Mexican, said.

"Speak, Tiny."

"Have you thought that the guy we've gotten the guns from could be setting us up?"

Franco thought about that for a few seconds, then shook his head.

"Nada, homes. How would he know where the guns were kept? The plug Toker got us is a blessing, and we need to keep our relationship with him smooth."

"Just a thought," Tiny said.

"Well, keep thinking. That goes for all of you." Franco headed to his car, followed by two of his homeboys he always kept by his side for security. He stopped and looked back at his homeboys and couldn't believe one of them was a snitch. Then he called out to Toker to come to him.

"What's up, Jefe?"

"You don't think your boy could be setting us up, do you?"

"No way, Jefe. Hot Shot ain't no cop. Like you said, how would he know where you kept the guns? The snitch has to be someone who knows where the guns are," Toker said as calmly as he could.

Franco nodded in agreement, turned, and left Toker standing there feeling relieved.

***

Hot Shot was in a dark place and needed to keep his head right. His heart was hurting. He needed to murder Franco like yesterday. He was becoming more and more frustrated every day he let Franco breathe. He got out of bed and told Cotton they were skipping their workout because he had something else to do. He grabbed his keys and left the house. He got into his car and drove to Inglewood Cemetery. Tears were sliding down his face the closer he got to the tomb where his mother, father, and little brother's bodies were laid to rest. He felt a clenching around his heart and thought he was having a heart attack. Slowly, he took a few deep breaths to calm himself down. The tears continued to flow as he said a silent prayer and stared at each of his family's names on their headstones. Then his eyes went back to his father's headstone, and he started talking to the headstone as if he were talking to his father.

"Dad, I miss y'all so much it hurts. I think back daily to every life lesson you gave me. I'm trying to be the best man I can be. My job has me doing good, yet I'm doing bad in the name of good. Is that contradictory?

Because of my job, I've found the people responsible for taking y'all away from me. I need vengeance in order to continue with my life right. You always told me family first and always to be there for your family. Protect your family at all costs. You always taught me that I should live my life as best as I can by God's rules. How can I do that when I murder the people responsible for taking my family away from me? How can I move forward with my life if I don't violate one of God's rules? Thou shall not kill. But I have killed. I've murdered men while in the military. I've murdered men by doing my job and never once felt as if I was breaking one of God's rules because I was fighting for our country and doing my job. Not once have I hesitated when it came to killing them.

Why is it so hard for me to push the line and kill this man? The man that gave the order to have y'all murdered. I may not be able to get the men that killed y'all, but I definitely can get the man who gave the order to have it done. Yet, I haven't done it. Why? Are you telling me from above not to kill this man? I'm so confused even though I know what must be done. I'll never be a good man to my wife or friends if this is not taken care of. I'll have a bad attitude and get angry, which could lead to bad decisions. Bad decisions in my line of work could end up having me killed. It's like I know what I must do, yet I haven't done it. Help me, Daddy, help me, please," Hot Shot pleaded and continued to weep. He wiped away his tears, then turned his eyes toward his brother's headstone . . . and his voice hardened.

"This is all your fault, Jeremy. If you hadn't wanted to be a damn drug dealer, you'd be alive. For the life of me, I don't understand what made you get into the drug game. What the hell were you thinking? I'm mad at you. I love you and miss you so much, but I'll never forgive you for what you've done. It's my burden to carry, and I will do what I must to keep my sanity."

He stood and kissed each headstone, then went back to his car, still crying. Once he started his car, the tears stopped. He wiped his face and took a deep breath. He felt better, but he knew if he didn't kill Franco, this bout of depression would return. There was no way in hell he would be depressed after murdering Franco, and that thought gave him solace.

"Girl, I love California. A bitch making some dollars and getting some good dick in sunny California. What more could a bitch ask for?" Lola said as she sat on Nola's bed, watching her sister as she hung up the clothes they had bought at the mall earlier.

"You are crazy; you know that, right? You are welcome to stay with us as long as you want, sister. But if you're thinking about staying out here for good, then you need to start looking for a place of your own to live," Nola said as she sat on the bed next to her sister.

"I was thinking about that. I wonder if Cotton would want to shack up with me. What do you think?"

"You're feeling Cotton like that, huh?"

"Indeed. That boy dick game is on *super* point."

"TMI. The dick good, I get that, but other than the dick, are you two compatible with living in the same house? Living here together isn't the same as sharing a place together, Lola."

"I know what you're saying, sister. I dig Cotton too. The sex is what makes our relationship so good. We talk, and we have a lot in common."

"If you don't, knock it off. What the hell do y'all have in common other than sexing each other every chance y'all can?"

"I'm serious, Nola. We talk about a lot of stuff. We both like to dress and look good at all times. That Texas boy is serious when it comes to his gear. And you know how I am when it comes to looking good. He always smells good, and his cologne game is above average. I know he talks to several bitches out here, and I don't have any problem with that. Shit, once I find a nigga worthy, I'm going to get my fuck on too."

"So, you want to stay out here with Cotton and get a place with him, and you both will fuck around on each other? That's crazy. You're nutso, Lola."

"No, I'm not, Nola. It's called having an open relationship. One thing we will never argue about is cheating. So take that element out of the relationship, and it's all good. We come and go as we please, and everybody is happy. You know I'm not the bitch that can be locked down."

"I can't believe that you have convinced yourself that Cotton would be open to having an open relationship with you."

"Why not?"

"Because though he won't admit it, Cotton is digging you more than he'll admit. No way in hell would he want to live with you and have an open relationship. That's why I think you should rethink shit. Talk to him and feel him out. I'm willing to bet he says no to your idea. He likes you too much."

"I like him too, and that's why I think he'd go for it. He can still fuck with all the bitches he wants but have the baddest bitch at home ready to fuck him good whenever he wants," Lola said matter-of-factly.

"If you say so. I don't agree with you, so we will see. But if you're going to stay here, who's going to take care of the ranch?"

"I can always fly back and look over things. I can pay the bills online, so taking care of the ranch won't be a problem. You act like you don't want me to stay out here with you. If that's the case, say so, and I'll go back home," Lola said with sadness.

"Now, you know damn well I don't have a problem with you staying with me. I just don't care for the situation with you and Cotton. But whatever you do, I got your back, sister."

Lola smiled and said, "I know, sister. I love you so much. I'll figure it out with Cotton and get back at you."

"No worries." Nola heard someone downstairs and said, "I think your boo is home."

"Let me go down there and see how he feels about the move shit."

"There's no rush, Lola."

"I know, but I still want to see what he's on," Lola said and went downstairs to talk to Cotton about them getting a place together. When she went downstairs, she saw Cotton sitting on the couch watching the news on TV.

"What's up, baby?" he asked when he saw her.

"Nothing much. I was talking to Nola, and she asked me about my plans. I was thinking about staying out here and getting my own place. What do you think about that, baby?"

"Fuck fuck fuck," Cotton quietly said to himself. He knew it was coming and had mixed emotions about Lola staying out here. But if she got her own place, it might just work.

"That's cool, boo. Where do you want to get your spot?"

"I don't know yet. I'm still trying to decide. Nothing is set in stone. I still gotta find some more people to make sure I got consistent money coming in."

"Right. You know shit out here ain't like Dallas. You gotta pay outta the ass out here."

"I know; that's crazy."

"Yeah, you're paying for this California sunshine and the Pacific. That's why I haven't been rushing to get my own spot. As long as Hot Shot is cool with me staying here, I'm good."

"Eventually, you're going to get your own place?"

"Yeah, just not anytime soon."

"Why don't you get a place with me? That way, we'll have our own and get out of Hot Shot and Nola's space."

Cotton thought about what she said and weighed the pros and cons of her suggestion. It would be cool to have his own place. Lola is supercool, and, of course, the sex was great. But would it work? That's the main question. He could still play the females he messes with because they won't know he has a place. This just might work.

"I don't know, boo. You think we're ready to make that kinda step?"

"If you're ready, I'm ready, baby. But baby, I'm no fool. I know you got a few bitches you fuck with out here, and in no way would I expect you to drop them and be only with me. So, we'll have an open relationship. You can do you, and I can do me, but when we get home, it's all about us."

"Are you serious?"

"Very."

"An open relationship as in you fuck with other men?"

"Right."

"I need to think about that, Lola. I'm not feeling you fucking with other men. If we do this, we got to do it as a couple. Fuck that open relationship shit."

Lola smiled. "You want us to be a couple, Cotton?"

"Honestly, I don't know. I do know I'm not with an open relationship get-down. Like you said, there's no rush, so let me think on it. If we do it, we do it as a couple, you being all mine, though."

"That's cool. Let me know when you figure it out, baby."

"Facts," Cotton said as he once again wondered if he wanted to live with Lola and be in a relationship. Their relationship has been all about sex. If they moved in together, shit would be different. Love might creep in, and that's a definite no-no. Damn, is love trying to enter his life? *There's no room for love in my life. Period,* he thought.

Chapter Twenty-two

Lola was laughing as she counted the money out for Hot Shot. Cotton frowned because Lola went to meet Fabian without letting him know so he could watch her back like Hot Shot told her. She saw the frown on his face and shook her head, hoping he didn't tell Hot Shot what she did. However, her hopes were in vain.

"You know she went and got with Fabian without me, Boss man."

Hot Shot and Nola stared at Lola, waiting for her to defend herself. Lola finished counting out the fifteen thousand she made with Fabian, sat back in her seat, and waited to get scolded.

"Lola, I see you getting the money, and that's a definite plus. I prefer safety over money, though. I asked you—no, I *told* you to let Cotton get your back when you deal with that dude. I expect you to do as I tell you. This is for your own safety, Lola," Hot Shot said.

"First off, I appreciate you wanting me to be safe. Second, I was waiting for Cotton to return, but he took too long, so I went and got the money before it got dark. And last, I've dealt with Fabian four times. I don't feel threatened by him, so why would I miss getting the money?"

"Did you not hear what Boss man said? It's about being *safe*," Cotton screamed as he stood and left the house, slamming the door behind him.

"Damn, is it *that* serious for that fool to yell at me?"

Hot Shot didn't say anything because he knew why Cotton was so emotional. Nola knew why Cotton screamed at her sister. Typically, if a man shouted at her sister, she would have gone off instantly, but she didn't this time because she knew Cotton really cared for her sister and appreciated him for it.

"Lola, can't you see that Cotton loves you, girl?" asked Nola.

"I know he's feeling me, sister, but love? Come on."

"The last time Cotton was in love, he lost his girlfriend."

"Lost?"

"Yes, sister, *lost*. As in, she killed herself after being raped by some of those South Dallas fools."

"Aww, that's sad."

"It is. It's obvious he has been fighting, but no one can fight loving a person after so long, no matter how much he doesn't want to. So, you'll have to decide what you're gonna do with his love, Lola."

"Wow."

"You need to heed what I tell you, Lola, or we're going to dead you getting down out here. I've seen how things can be all good with someone out here and then go bad just as fast as it started. Not saying Fabian is like that, but a man can try to rock you to sleep by getting at you for more and more meth, then call you for a bigger order, and then get at you bad and take everything. He might let you make it or say forget it and hurt you. No one could get revenge for you because you would be dead. I told you it's different here in California," Hot Shot said seriously.

"I understand all of that, Shot, but it's like I told y'all, Fabian wants this pussy so bad he'd never do me dirty. The streets are the same from state to state, Shot. I know how to maneuver in any street setting. I know how to judge a slimy person, and if I felt any threat from Fabian, I'd adjust accordingly. I hear you, though."

Hot Shot sighed and stared at his wife, giving her an exasperated look. Nola understood the look and frowned.

"Sister, either you're going to do it how Shot wants you to, or it all stops. There's nothing else to talk about," Nola said as she got to her feet and went into the kitchen, ending the discussion.

"It's like that, Shot?"

"Yes, Lola, it's like that." Hot Shot went upstairs, leaving Lola alone downstairs thinking. She understood how they felt. She would do as they asked of her. She was thinking about what they said about Cotton loving her. Love wasn't what she needed or wanted. She was all about sex and having fun. They were having a good time. Why would Cotton go and catch feelings? As she thought about him loving her, she had to smile. But *love?* Damn, that's an entirely different animal. Something foreign to her. She sat back and thought about it, and as she was smiling, she realized that she could love Cotton. *Now, ain't that some shit?* she said to herself.

Cotton was so mad that he could barely see as he drove to Long Beach to visit Yolanda. He needed to check himself and his feelings for Lola. He loved her more each day, but that had to stop. There was no way he would be with her if she couldn't obey the rules regarding her selling meth to Fabian. He wouldn't be able to take it if something happened to her. He thought back to when he watched the love of his life, Meosha, blow her brains out. He had been so devastated. There wouldn't be any coming back from that another time. So he had to pull all his feelings in and do what he did. He smiled and thought about Yolanda's slim, thick body. The best way to get ahold of his feelings was to get with Yolanda and fuck her brains out on a daily if he had too. And that was a task he didn't mind taking on.

As Cotton got off the 710 Freeway, he got a call from Hakeem, Yolanda's brother.

"What's good, bro?"

"It's all good, Cotton. I need to make a bigger order, though. You in pocket?"

"What you trying to get?"

"I need 5,000 oxy pills."

"Like that, huh?"

"Yeah, like that. Can you handle that for me?"

"Let me make a call, and I'll hit you back. I'm almost at your sister's house. I'll hit you when I get there."

"OK, cool. I'm at Yolanda's house now. See you when you get here," Hakeem said as he ended the call.

Cotton called Hot Shot and told him what he needed to get for Hakeem.

"Let me call JT. I think it's time to put the green light on Fabian and Hakeem. It's time to take down Fabian if we want to protect Lola's hardheaded ass."

"For real, Boss man. I don't give a fuck what she does or how she does it. If she ain't gon' listen, then that's on her ass."

"Stop it. I know you're feeling her, and there's nothing wrong with that, Cotton. You don't have to front with me, bro. I know the business. I'll hit you back in a few to let you know when we have the order for your mans."

"That's what's up," Cotton said, ending the call as he pulled in front of Yolanda's house. When he saw her baby daddy, he shook his head and thought, *I am so not in the mood to deal with this clown. If Doug wants the smoke, I'm going to give him all he can take,* Cotton said to himself as he put the pistol in the small of his back and got out of his truck. He saw Hakeem talking to Doug and headed in their direction.

"What it do, gentlemen?" Cotton said as he shook hands with Hakeem and stared at Doug.

"You don't have to worry, Cotton. Doug not tripping," Hakeem said with a serious look.

"I'm not tripping. It's all good."

"What's up? You got the green light yet?"

"Nah, waiting on the callback."

Yolanda came outside with her son on her hip and gave him to his father. Doug smiled at his boy and kissed him on the cheeks. The little boy was as cute as can be, and Cotton smiled. Yolanda gave Doug a small tote bag with her son's things.

"I'll bring him back in the morning," Doug told her.

"That's fine," she replied, turning toward Cotton and frowning. "Well, look at the stranger. I almost gave up on seeing you again."

Cotton smiled and said, "Come on, baby, you know better than that."

"Do I?"

"You know you do."

"Humph. Come on in the house. Y'all don't need to be standing out there like y'all not welcomed."

Cotton followed Hakeem into Yolanda's house and took a seat. Yolanda sat on his lap, and Cotton wrapped his arms around her and said, "You know I've been missing you, baby. For real. I let my business get out of hand, and I had to stop and look at it for a few minutes. I was letting my business control me instead of me controlling my business. That won't happen again, baby. My word," he said, and for some reason, he saw Lola's pretty face. Instantly, he shook the thought of her out of his mind. *Damn, I'm tripping,* he thought.

"You better keep your word, boy. I'm not playing with you," Yolanda said and gave him a kiss with a little tongue action.

"You two can wait until I leave with all that smooching shit," Hakeem said, smiling. Before Cotton could respond, his phone rang. He moved Yolanda off his lap and pulled out his phone. He smiled as Hot Shot told him he would have 5,000 oxy pills in two days. He ended the call and told Hakeem he would be ready for him in two days.

"That's what's up. Can we meet over here, Yolanda?"

"I don't have a problem with that as long as I get broken off by both of you."

"I don't know about your brother, but I'm definitely going to break you off, baby."

"I'm not talking about just the dick, boy," she said and punched him lightly on the arm.

"I know, baby. I'll have some coin for you."

"Thank you, baby."

"I got you too, sis."

"That's what's up. OK, Hakeem. I don't have my son for the rest of the night, and your business has been handled. You can leave now so I can handle some business of my own."

Hakeem started laughing as he left the house.

"You ready, baby?" she asked Cotton as she stood and pulled off the T-shirt she was wearing.

"You damn right I'm ready, boo."

She took him to her bedroom and handled her business.

Chapter Twenty-three

Hot Shot watched Nola get dressed and couldn't take the smile off his face. He loved his wife and everything about her. She was street savvy, intelligent, sexy, and drop-dead gorgeous. Nola saw her husband staring at her body and began to tease him a little bit by bending over, acting as if she was fixing her stockings, and he moaned loudly.

She laughed and asked, "Is something wrong, honey?"

"You know what's wrong. Keep playing with me, and your outing with your sister will be canceled."

"Don't worry, honey. I'll take care of you later when I come home."

"If I'm asleep, by all means, wake me up."

"Gotcha."

Hot Shot laughed as he stood and left the bedroom so she could finish getting dressed. He went downstairs and saw Cotton talking to someone on the phone, so he went into the kitchen, grabbed a bottle of beer, and went back into the living room. He didn't have anything to do, so he was just chilling at home while Nola and Lola went to a restaurant in Malibu. He wasn't in the mood to do anything. He was concerned about the disappearance of Franco. He watched his house for three days, and Franco, obviously, was staying someplace other than home. He called Toker, who had no information for him.

"I don't know where the hell he at, Shot. No one has heard from him in a few days. When I get word, I'll let you know for sure."

"Do you know where he took that last load of weapons?"

"Nope."

"OK, stay safe, and be sure to get at me when you see him."

"Say less."

Hot Shot sat on the couch and heard Cotton tell whomever he was on the phone with that he would get with them later and ended the call. Then finally, he turned to Hot Shot and shook his head.

"I'm getting tired of going back-and-forth with these women out here. One minute, they were with the program, but as soon as I put this dick on them, they wanted me to be with them all the damn time. There's not enough time in a day to be fucking with them all the time."

"Ah, I see . . . the life of a playa."

"I'm serious, Boss man. These women have gotten on my nerves."

"You ever thought about being with just *one* woman? It will still be stressful, but at least you won't have multiple headaches—just one," Hot Shot said, laughing.

"You know the answer to that question. Meosha was my forever. I'll never be with one woman. Love hurts, and I never want to feel like I felt after losing her."

"I understand, Cotton. What happened to Meosha was a sad situation, but you can't let that incident stop you from finding real love. She would not want you living that way. If you find a woman you feel is worthy of your love, you should try it. If it doesn't work out, at least you tried. Don't just give up on love, bro."

"You talking about Lola, huh?"

Hot Shot shrugged. "Lola or whatever woman you messing with. Don't shut love down, bro. Life's too short."

"I feel you, Boss man. I'm digging Lola more than I ever thought I would. I respect a strong woman and all that shit, but her mouth and attitude like she knows every damn thing gets on my nerves, making me wonder how I really feel about her. She's nothing like Nola. They may look alike, but they damn sure ain't the same."

"You got that right, but don't get it twisted, bro. Nola is a lot like Lola. She gets on my nerves too. All women have that trait. You have to be able to accept some faults because no one is perfect."

"Facts."

"You'll be all right, bro. On another note, I'm picking up that package for you tomorrow. JT will give the green light on your man and Fabian later this week. Time to bring this mission to an end."

"That's cool. What about Franco?"

"That's on hold. He's vanished, but he'll pop up again. When he does, we will put an end to it and get ready to take our talents on the road."

"Yeah? Where are we going?"

"I don't know, but I told JT it was time to get me out of Cali. Wherever we go, it will be better than out here."

"Will Nola join us?"

"That, bro, is a good question. She's going to want to, and I won't front. I'd love to have her with me, but I don't think it would work. We'll be handling business. It's bad enough I got you to worry about. It will be even worse if I let her come with us."

"What you mean, 'got me to worry about'? I carry my load."

"For some reason, you always seem to find the bullshit, bro. You know it's true."

"Right. But I do be handling my business, right?"

"Facts."

"What will you tell Nola when it's time for us to bounce?"

"That she will have to wait until we have everything set up."

With a grin, Cotton asked, "Do you *really* think that will work?"

"Probably not."

They both laughed.

"What are you two jokers laughing about?" Lola asked as she stepped into the living room, looking pretty in a floral print skirt and some bright pink heels on her petite feet. Then Nola came downstairs looking just as pretty as her sister, wearing a cream-colored skirt with black heels. They were indeed a stunning set of twins.

"OK, put your tongues back in your mouths. Y'all act like y'all never saw us before," Nola said as she came to her husband and kissed him on the cheek. "See you later, baby."

"You better believe it," Hot Shot said with a huge smile.

"Be good out there, lady," Cotton said to Lola.

"You need to be telling me to be good when I get back, *not* when I'm gone, sugar," Lola said and gave him a kiss with some tongue. He moaned, and she laughed as they made their exit.

Both men smiled as the door closed behind the twins.

"I don't know what the fuck I'm going to do, Boss man."

"Follow your heart. If it's meant to be, it will be, bro."

"Say less."

Chapter Twenty-four

Hot Shot called Cotton and informed him that he was on his way home with the oxy for Hakeem. He told him to make sure he told Lola that he had what she needed for Fabian as well.

"I'm going to roll with her this time to make sure she's straight."

"That's a good idea, Boss man."

"You make sure you watch your six too. The same rule applies to you too."

"Don't I know it? My locator is on, and if it looks sticky, I have no problem bouncing. But I don't think Hakeem would try me, especially with me fucking with his sister."

"Don't take that for granted. You never know what a man will do, especially if times get desperate. Situations can change suddenly, and that you can never account for. What you can do is watch yourself and stay ready so you won't have to *get* ready."

"Facts," Cotton said as he ended the call and texted Hakeem to see if he was ready to meet him at his sister's house. It took a few minutes before Hakeem replied that he was ready and would be at Yolanda's place in an hour. Cotton responded that he would see him then.

After that, Cotton entered the kitchen and saw Lola bending over in the refrigerator. He smiled as he snuck up behind her, slapped her lightly on her ass, and said, "Hey, baby."

When Nola turned around with a frown on her face, he screamed, "Oh shit! My bad, Nola. I thought you were Lola."

"I know what you thought, fool."

"I mean, for real. Y'all gotta wear some name tags or some shit. This keeps a man confused around this damn house."

They both started laughing. Lola heard their laughter and came into the kitchen to see what was funny.

"What the hell are you two laughing at?"

"Your man slapped me on my ass thinking I was you."

"What? Now that *is* funny."

"Yeah, he said we need to wear some name tags so he won't be so damn confused." That caused them all to laugh.

"Well, I'll leave you two, so y'all can whip up some bomb breakfast for a hungry Black man."

"You better tell your woman to make you something. I got a nail appointment," Nola said as she exited.

"Are you going to hook me up, baby?"

"I got you, boo. You sit right there, and I'll put something together for you. I want to talk to you anyway."

"About what?"

"Us."

"What about us?"

"I want you to be totally honest with me, Cotton."

"I will."

Lola grabbed some bacon and eggs out of the refrigerator, turned, set them on the counter, and asked, "How do you feel about me? I mean, how do you *really* feel about me, Cotton?"

"I love you," Cotton said . . . just as surprised as Lola was to hear those words come out of his mouth.

"Don't be playing with me, boy. I'm serious."

"I'm not playing with you, Lola. I not only love you, but I'm also in love with you, and I want you to be my woman."

"If I hadn't asked, when were you going to make me aware of this information, sir?"

"I don't know. I've been going back and forth with this for a good minute now. You asked, and I felt the time was right to let you know how I feel."

"Wow."

"Your turn. How do *you* feel about *me?*"

"I don't want to hurt you."

"Give it to me straight. I'm a big boy. I can take it," he said, feeling like a fool for admitting how he felt about her.

"I'm in love with you, Cotton."

He felt so relieved he almost jumped out of his seat. However, he didn't trust how his voice would sound, so he simply nodded.

"Like I said, I don't want to hurt you because I never thought I could be in love with any man. This shit is new to me, and I just don't know what to do."

"All we can do is take it one day at a time and let it be what it will be. It doesn't take a rocket scientist to know how to love a person."

"Right. I don't want to take the fun out of what we got by being all serious and shit. I already see you as a clingy type, which is cute, but sometimes, I like to do me the way I do me. I might wear something edgy that makes me feel sexy, and I don't want you with a hair up your ass behind it. Just like I don't be tripping when you be texting those other bitches all the damn time. That bothers me, but I don't say shit. If we gon' do this, we got to be able to do it, yet remain focused on the boundaries."

"Yes, boundaries."

"You like fucking other bitches; I get that. You can keep talking to your bitches, but you need to include me. Shit, I might want to get freaky with the bitch *and* you."

"Stop fucking playing," he said, grinning.

"I'm serious. I'm not all stuck up like my sister. I'm with the freaky shit."

He frowned and said, "I'm not with fucking you with another man."

Laughing, she said, "Oh, I know, honey. Like I was saying, you can still do you. Just make me a part of it. If you see me on one, and I'm being flirty with it, don't trip. That's me being me. I will keep to our boundaries and not fuck with no man. See, it's important to me that if we are going to do this and make it long term that we be able to live in our truth. We do this right, baby, and we'll be together for the long ride."

"Damn. I want you to always keep it real with me. No lies, no games, and be totally honest at all times."

"Right, and that goes both ways."

"That's that then. We are one from this point forward."

"Yep. Let me hurry up with your breakfast so we can go get our fuck on to seal the deal," she said, laughing.

"Fuck that breakfast. Come here," he said as he pulled her into his arms.

They shared a long kiss. Then he turned her around, pulled up the sleep shirt she was wearing, and eased his dick inside her wet pussy. He bent her on the counter and began pounding away in her hot pussy.

A few minutes later, they both came so loud that Nola yelled downstairs at them, swearing they better not be fucking in the damn kitchen. They held each other, both panting heavily and laughing.

Hot Shot came home and heard Lola and Cotton in their room, laughing. He smiled, set the two packages for them on the coffee table, and went upstairs to see what his wife was doing. Nola was in the shower, so he sat on the bed and thought about Franco. *Where are you, Franco? Don't hide, you motherfucker. I'm ready to take your life, you coward.* Then he lay on the bed with these thoughts.

Nola came out of the shower and saw him on the bed with his eyes closed. She smiled at him as she slipped on a pair of shorts and a T-shirt. He opened his eyes and stared at her.

"What's on your mind, baby?" she asked as she sat on the bed.

"It's all good, baby, but Franco has disappeared, and it's bothering me. I'm ready to dead this whole situation. Now that I'm ready, this fool has gone MIA on me. That's funny, but it is what it is."

"He ain't going to be gone too long, baby. So don't let it stress you."

"Not stressed at all, baby. I just think it's funny that I'm ready, and then he vanishes. Anyway, what are you doing for the day?"

"No plans yet. Trying to see if Lola wants to do something. You know, we're having fun getting to know our way around Cali."

"That's cool. I just got a sack for Lola, so she'll meet Fabian today. I'm going to watch her six, so she won't try to do it alone."

"Good idea."

"Facts. Other than that, I won't be doing much. JT is pressing the go button on Fabian and the guy that Cotton has been dealing with, so that will be a done deal. I've been wondering why I haven't heard from Piru Pete. He was supposed to have gotten at me."

"I'm sure he will. No need to worry about stuff you can't control, baby, so relax."

"That's exactly what I intend on doing."

"Good. I'm about to make something to eat. You good?"

He closed his eyes and said, "Yes, baby, I'm good. Tell Lola to let me know when she plans on getting at Fabian."

"OK," Nola said as she left the bedroom. When she entered the kitchen, she saw Cotton sitting at the dining room table, and Lola was frying some bacon.

"What you two heathens doing?"

"We chilling, gurl. What's up with you?" Lola said as she continued cooking.

"I'm about to make a sandwich, then relax. Shot told me to tell you to let him know when you're going to meet Fabian. He said he's going to watch your back."

Lola rolled her eyes but didn't respond.

Cotton did. "That's good. Now, I can go get with Hakeem and get my business out of the way today."

"Y'all be making a big deal over nothing. That's so irritating."

"The rule is never to get caught slipping. Stop taking it personally. Boss man is that way with me too, baby."

"Yeah, OK."

Nola laughed, grabbed a piece of bacon, and promptly got her hand popped by her sister. "Ouch."

"Get your hands off this bacon. It's for me and my man. You better cook your own."

"Your man? Who's your man?"

"Me and Cotton made it official. We're in a relationship."

Nola stared at Cotton to see what he would say.

Cotton smiled and said, "That's right. We trying to give us a try."

"Well, look at y'all all boo'd up. That's cool. I'm happy for both of you."

"Thank you," they both said in unison.

Nola made something to eat and went back to the bedroom to see Hot Shot sound asleep. Then she went back downstairs so she could watch TV and relax.

Lola came out of the kitchen and went to get dressed so she could meet Fabian and make some more money. She was making some nice coins with Fabian, but she wanted more. She needed to find more people to deal with. Fabian was getting more and more meth from her. That was cool, but the greed factor had kicked in, and she *needed* more customers. More money, more money was on her mind.

Cotton entered the bedroom and started getting dressed so he could handle his business with Hakeem. They both had money on their minds as they went and shared a shower together.

Chapter Twenty-five

Nola was bored, so when she saw Hot Shot was about to leave and watch Lola's back as she dealt with Fabian, she told Hot Shot she was going with him. As they followed Lola to the agreed-upon spot for her to meet Fabian, Nola had a funny feeling, and she didn't know why. She reached into the waistband of her sweatpants and gripped her pistol, praying she wouldn't have to use it. If she even *thought* her sister was in danger, she knew she would kill any and everyone around her sibling. She tried to shake those thoughts as they followed Lola.

Hot Shot felt the tension coming off his wife in waves. Her silence was the first sign. Then when he noticed how she gripped her gun, he began to feel edgy. The last thing he wanted was to get into a gunfight in broad daylight in the city of Hawthorne. He told himself everything would be all good and continued driving.

Once they made it to Ralph's grocery store, Hot Shot watched as Lola parked her car in the back of the parking lot. He bypassed her and parked his car in the back as well, but he backed in, so he had Lola right in his sights. Then he sat back, relaxed, and waited.

"Everything is going to be OK, baby."

"I know, Shot, but there's something different about watching my sister making a drug deal. If we were in Texas, I wouldn't even think nothing about it. But I just got a funny feeling and can't shake it."

"Be easy, baby, and try to remain calm."

"Say less."

Lola saw how Hot Shot parked a few cars from her and backed in, so they were looking right at her. She shook her head and felt like they were really overreacting. After all, Fabian was putty in her hands. He would never try any grimy shit with her. He wanted to get the pussy too bad to do some weak shit. Plus, she thought he wasn't that type of dude as she waited for him to arrive.

She sat up straight when she saw Fabian's black BMW pull in next to her car. She was so focused on him that she didn't pay any attention to the blue Cadillac Escalade pull into the parking space right next to her. But although she was unaware of it, Nola and Hot Shot carefully watched the scene unfold.

Lola was staring at Fabian, waiting for him to get in her car like he always did, but this time, he was staring straight ahead. Perplexed, she rolled down the passenger window and tried getting his attention. Everything from that point happened so fast that she didn't register what was going on . . . until she heard the gunshots. Hot Shot and Nola had begun firing at the two guys who jumped out of the blue SUV. Both men ducked and returned fire. Hot Shot saw Fabian speed out of the parking lot. He let a few more shots go and ducked behind a car while Nola was still running straight at the blue vehicle, firing away. Lola snapped out of it and immediately sped out of the parking lot, giving chase to Fabian.

"You bitch motherfucker! I'm going to kill your ass," she screamed as she flew down Hawthorne Boulevard.

Hot Shot made it to Nola's side and snatched her back just as she was about to be in front of the SUV. He pulled her behind him as he slowly approached the back of the vehicle, where both men were on the ground, moaning in pain from their gunshot wounds. Nola began kicking both men, screaming at the top of her lungs.

"You bitch-ass, punk-ass cowards tried to rob my sister. Fuck-boy-ass bitches, y'all about to die!" She raised her pistol and began pulling the trigger over and over and over. Thank God she had run out of bullets, or both men would have been dead. Hot Shot grabbed her, picked up where Nola had left off, and began kicking the wounded men. Then he snatched one to his feet and screamed in his face to tell them where Fabian lived.

"He lives in Long Beach, man. Please, let me go."

"Where in Long Beach?"

"Right on the corner of Cherry and Carson, 1124 Cherry. Man, please, let me go."

Hot Shot slapped the man with his gun, knocking him to the ground, screaming.

Nola was pistol-whipping the other man so severely that Hot Shot just knew she was killing him. He snatched his wife off her feet and began jogging back to his car. Once they were inside the vehicle, he sped out of the parking lot, hearing police sirens screaming, and headed toward Ralph's. Nola was still screaming, and he was trying to calm her down so they could get their bearings.

"Baby, calm down and focus. Call Lola and see where she went."

Hearing her sister's name seemed to calm her enough to grab her phone and call Lola. When Lola answered, Nola asked, "Where the fuck are you, sister?"

"I just got on the 105 East Fwy, following that fuck-boy-ass Fabian." Nola had her phone on speaker, so Hot Shot heard what she said.

"Fall back, Lola. There's no need to follow him. I know where he's going. I have his address. Don't chase him. We will get his ass, so fall back."

"Fuck that shit, Shot. I'm going to get this bitch myself."

"Lola, you are rolling at a high speed on the freeway with two fucking kilos of meth. Are you trying to go to fucking jail? Calm the fuck down and listen to what I'm telling you. I have the address to where he's going. You will be able to get him—my word. So slow down and calm down."

"Sister, listen to what Shot is telling you. Please, gurl, you know damn well you can't go to jail," Nola screamed.

As her sister's voice registered, her words hit home. Lola was extremely claustrophobic. There was no way she could be put in a jail cell. She would lose her mind. Her foot eased off the gas pedal, and she watched as Fabian extended his lead and was soon out of sight.

"I sure hope y'all ain't lying because I'm losing his ass."

"Where are you now, Lola?" asked Hot Shot.

"I'm turning on the 710 South."

"Is that the direction Fabian went?"

"Yes."

"OK. Good. Listen to me and listen good. Take the 710 to the Del Amo exit and turn left. Take Del Amo to Long Beach Boulevard and park at the Shell gas station. We're behind you and should be there ten minutes or so after you. Then we will go see Fabian and handle up."

Calm now, Lola said, "OK, Shot."

"Are you OK, sister?" asked Nola.

"Yeah, I'm good. Mad as fuck, but I'm good. I was scared as fuck because I didn't know what the hell was happening. All I heard was gunshots when I looked up and saw it was y'all that was doing the shooting. I instantly knew some shit went wrong, and that's when that fuck boy Fabian sped off, so I went right behind his ass. Thank God y'all was there. Lord have mercy."

Hot Shot wanted to say something but thought better of it when he saw the "not now" look his wife gave him. So instead, he grabbed his phone and called Cotton to let him know what happened. When he finished, Cotton was furious.

"Where are y'all at now, Boss man?"

"We're going to Long Beach to meet up with Lola at the Shell on Del Amo and Long Beach Boulevard. Then we going to Fabian's house to pay him a visit."

"I'm headed to Long Beach to get with Hakeem, but I'll meet y'all at the Shell," Cotton said as he made a quick exit and headed toward where his woman was.

As soon as Hot Shot stopped his car behind Lola's, his wife jumped out and ran to her sister. The twins held each other tightly, weeping. Their bond was so tight that they would die for each other. Hot Shot stayed back and let them get their emotions in order. Cotton pulled into the Shell ten minutes later, jumped out of his truck, and ran to Lola.

"You good, baby?" he asked as he grabbed her and squeezed her in his arms.

"Yes, baby, I'm OK, thanks to my sister and Hot Shot. They were going to rob me, baby. I feel so lame right now. Ugh."

"Don't worry about that. It's all good now. You're all right, and now you get to see how me and Shot get down."

"Facts," said Shot.

"Fuck you talking about *I* get to see *you and Shot* get down? Y'all about to see how *me and my sister* get down."

"Facts," said Nola looking directly into her husband's eyes, daring him to utter a word with her fiery glare.

He smiled to diffuse his wife and said, "Fuck all the talking about it. Let's go *be* about it."

"Say less," three answered in unison.

Chapter Twenty-six

Fabian pulled into his garage, then went inside his house, scared out of his mind. *Why in the fuck did I let them fools talk me into letting them rob Lola?* he thought as he went to the bar and poured a shot of vodka. After two more shots, he calmed down and wondered if his cousins were OK. They weren't answering their phones, so he feared the worst. When he saw Lola's sister and some guy charging toward them shooting, he got the hell out of Dodge as fast as he could. Now that he was home, he felt safe . . . but he was still spooked. He thanked God for Lola not knowing where he lived. He asked her several times to come over, and she declined every time, and he was so thankful for that now.

He went to the back room with the bottle of vodka in hand. Then he sat down and replayed everything in his head. He knew he shouldn't have tried that shit. Everything was going smoothly until greed took over. He ran his mouth, so he couldn't blame anyone but himself. He was bragging to his cousins that he finally found a consistent plug with the meth, and they were good. He slipped when he told them Lola was a girl. They instantly started pressing him to let them rob her, and he gave in, and the rest was history. Now, here he was, wondering if his cousins were alive or in jail.

Fuck.

He took another shot of vodka and lay back in his recliner . . . when all hell suddenly broke loose. The back door burst open. Fabian couldn't believe his eyes when he saw two men enter his house, followed by Lola and her twin sister. He knew he was fucked, but how the fuck did they know where he lived? Suddenly, he knew the answer to that question. His cousins told them. *Oh God, please don't let these people kill me,* he prayed silently.

"You bitch-ass fuck boy. You thought you was going to rob me? You stupid fuck," Lola screamed as she slapped Fabian in the head with her pistol.

Cotton went throughout the house to make sure they were alone. When he returned, he nodded at Hot Shot. Then Hot Shot tied Fabian to one of his dining room chairs. Once he was secure, Lola went in again and began repeatedly pistol-whipping Fabian. Hot Shot was impressed. She was working Fabian so badly that Cotton had to stop her before she killed him. Nola went into the house and began searching for money. She returned to the back room with a frustrated look on her face.

Lola slapped Fabian again and said, "Now, bitch, where is your money? You don't give it up, you're a dead man, I swear to God."

"It's in the closet under my shoe boxes, in a floor safe. Combination 3223," Fabian said with blood gushing out of his mouth.

Nola left, then returned a few minutes later carrying a small bag filled with cash. Then she left the house to make sure no police were coming. She looked inside the bag and saw it was close to $300,000. "Not bad," she said and sat back in her seat, waiting on the others to exit.

Hot Shot stopped Cotton from punching Fabian in the face. That was enough. Fabian would go to jail soon, and Lola and Cotton had hurt him sufficiently.

"Fabian, I need to know you won't be trying to find a way to get back at us. If you can't convince me, then you die. I feel the ass whooping you got plus the money we're taking is punishment enough. But I need to know if you're tough enough to try to get some get back. Talk to me."

Through busted lips, cracked teeth, and a broken nose, Fabian said, "I'm good. Y'all got that, so please don't kill me. I'm sorry for trying to rob Lola. Please don't kill me," he whined.

"OK, I believe you," Hot Shot said, then punched Fabian so hard that he was sure he broke Fabian's jaw. "Never *ever* fuck with my people again. If I even *think* you're trying to get back at any of my people, I'll come blow your brains out, bitch," Hot Shot said in a menacing tone. Then he turned around and walked out the door, followed by Lola and Cotton, leaving Fabian beaten and battered, crying like a baby.

Once outside, Hot Shot told Nola to ride back to their house with Lola. He was going to follow Cotton to handle the business with Hakeem.

"I'm good, Boss man. You can go on back to the house too."

"No. I'm following you," Hot Shot said with finality as he got inside his car.

Cotton knew not to say anything else. It was one of those days. Instead, he climbed into his truck and eased away from the curb. He texted Hakeem, letting him know he was eight minutes from Yolanda's house. Hakeem responded that he was already there. *Cool,* Cotton thought as he continued to drive, thinking about how much rage was inside him because of the Fabian situation. "These Cali fools are extra for real. They had the right one. If they want smoke, we will give them plenty," he muttered.

Soon, he saw Doug outside talking to Hakeem with two other guys. Now Cotton was cool that Hot Shot had decided to follow him. He didn't think anything would go down, but he was happy Hot Shot was there to watch his back while he handled his business. He put his pistol in the small of his back, grabbed the bag with the oxy, jumped out of his truck, and walked toward the four men.

"What's good, gentlemen?" Cotton said when he was standing in front of them.

"It's all good out here," Hakeem said as he shook hands with Cotton.

Cotton noticed how none of the men in front returned his greeting. So he pulled out his phone and texted Hot Shot.

Stay ready.

Hot Shot responded with, Say less.

What the hell is going on today? Everybody is trying to rob us, he thought.

"What's good? You ready to get this handled?"

"Yep," Hakeem answered as he turned and went inside the house. The three men waited for Cotton to enter the house first, but he waited them out until they relented and went inside before he entered.

"Good move, Cotton. Never let nobody get in position to cause you harm," Hot Shot said as he sat on his car across the street from where Cotton was.

After Cotton entered the house, he stared at the men trying to gauge their intentions. Their faces were dead-pan—not a smirk, anger, or mean mugging. He shrugged it off and went into the kitchen, where Hakeem counted the money. Cotton set the bag he was carrying full of oxy on the table.

"There you go, bro. I see you're getting your weight up," Cotton said.

"Yep. I gotta keep it poppin'. Now that I have a solid connection, I don't have to worry about going without oxy. These fools out here be iffy, and I don't have to worry about that, fucking with you."

"Say less."

Hakeem gave Cotton his money and said, "I'll be back at you in a few days, and I'll most likely double up then."

"Let me know, and I'll get at you ASAP. I'm out," Cotton said as he turned and left the kitchen. As he was walking past Doug and his homeboys, Cotton gave them a nod and said, "Y'all stay dangerous."

"Always, cuz," Doug said as he glared at Cotton.

Cotton laughed as he left the house.

Doug came out behind him and said, "Something funny, cuh? You know the only reason I ain't got at your ass is you cool with Hakeem."

Cotton started to say something but chose not to and kept walking toward his truck. As he opened the door, he saw Doug's two homeboys walking toward him. He pulled out his gun and said, "Today really is *not* a good day for you fools to try me."

"Oh, you a tough nigga with that pistol, huh?" said the taller of the two men.

"Yep. And if you keep at it, I'll show you I'm not scared to use it, so fall the fuck back."

Cotton got into his truck, sighed as he started the loud engine, and pulled away from the curb, laughing. He saw Hot Shot following him, and he was glad it didn't have to get ugly because two incidents in one day could've turned out bad for those Crips. All was well, but he knew eventually he would have to deal with Doug. He made a mental note to tell Hakeem not to have anyone around whenever he came to deal with him again.

Chapter Twenty-seven

Lola was steaming as she sat and listened to Hot Shot's "I told you so" lecture. She knew she had it coming but was really not feeling up to hearing it. He was right, though, she said to herself as she fumed. She couldn't believe Fabian had tried her like that. She slipped, and the slippers in this game fell. She was glad Hot Shot chose to come to watch her back. She really would have felt dumb if she had gotten robbed. Maybe the game out here *was* different, like Hot Shot said. *I'll leave this shit up to them, fall back, enjoy Cotton's money, and stay safe.* That thought made her smile, and Hot Shot took her smiling the wrong way.

"There's nothing funny about this situation, Lola. You put yourself in harm's way and the entire team. Everything went right, but what if it hadn't fallen that way? What if you would've gotten hurt—or worse? What if we had gotten caught up when we went to Fabian's house? We were lucky. But what about the next time you decide to go solo to handle your business? I set rules, not just to be in charge. I set the rules for our safety. I don't want any of y'all hurt or in jail. That complicates things, and I'm trying not to have any complications, Lola—none at all."

"I understand, Shot, and you don't have to worry about something like that ever happening again. I'm done. I want no part of the game out here in Cali. Not that I can't handle it, but I got too cocky and comfortable. And it almost cost me. I'm done."

Thank you, Lord, Nola said to herself.

Good, Cotton said to himself.

"OK, that's your call. If you try to get at it again, just make sure you follow the rules, and we'll be good."

"It's good that you want to fall back, baby. We got this out here. You just stay pretty, and we will handle this shit," Cotton said with a smile.

"The rules go for you too, Cotton. From what you told me, you almost had an issue with those Crips. So when you make your moves, you need to make sure one of us has your six. This isn't up for discussion either, bro."

"You got that, Boss man."

"Good. Everything is all good now, so we'll take this lesson and learn from it."

As he finished speaking, Hot Shot got a text from Piru Pete. So he called Pete to see what was on his mind since it's been a few weeks since he last heard from him.

"What's good, Pete?"

"It's been wild out here in Bompton, but it's all good. The homies had an issue getting their money together, but they're ready to move now."

"I was wondering because you had me make that order. It's cool, though. When you are trying to make it happen?"

"ASAP. The thing is, my homie who's putting up most of the money wants to come to the meeting spot when we exchange the guns."

"I don't have a problem with that. We can hook up tomorrow at 11:00 a.m. You'll meet my man at Tams again, and when he tells me it's all good, come to the back of the Food For Less parking lot so we can make the exchange."

"That's right, P. Bee you then," Pete said and ended the call.

"I was going to handle that move with Pete today since I still have the guns here, but I thought better of it. We've had enough activity for one day. Time to chill and relax."

"For real," Nola said as she stood and went upstairs with Hot Shot following behind her.

"What do you have on your plate for the rest of the day, baby?" Lola asked Cotton.

"Nothing. I'm still tripping off that shit with that clown Fabian. If something would've happened to you, I would've lost my mind, baby."

"Nothing happened, baby, so let it go. You won't have to worry about anything like that again. I'm out of the way, baby."

"Right. I'm hungry. Do you wanna go get something to eat?"

"Yeah, but I'm not in the mood to sit at a restaurant."

"Where do you want to go?"

"I want to go get one of those pastrami burritos from that fast-food place you took me to."

Cotton laughed and said, "You want some Louies? I thought you didn't like it the last time?"

"It grew on me the more I ate it. Either that or some chili cheese fries."

"Come on, then, baby. We're off to Compton."

Hot Shot and Nola were watching old movies on Netflix, both relaxed and relieved that everything was all good. Hot Shot had called JT and let him know what happened and told him it was definitely time to arrest Fabian and Hakeem. JT told him the calls had been made and everything would be handled in the next day or so. Hot Shot also told him about Piru Pete and how he was meeting him to sell the guns.

"That's good. Then we can put that right into effect. What about the I-13s?"

"Been real quiet."

"We put a dent into their operation, so I guess we can close this mission."

"I'll hit Toker and see if he has something new for me. If not, then I guess so."

"OK, son. You have a good evening, and I'll be in touch. I'll check with the director and see where he wants you to go for your next mission."

"That's cool because it's time to get out of here for a while."

"I bet it is, son. Talk to you soon," JT said and ended the call.

Nola stared at Hot Shot and asked, "Mission complete?"

"Yes."

"Where will the next mission take place?"

"I don't know yet. JT will get me that information soon."

"You *do* know I'm coming with you, right?"

"I don't know how that's going to work, baby. So we all pack up and go to the next state? We're involving your sister in our business now, and that's not a good look. So I think it would be better if you two stay here while Cotton and I go do what we do. I'll send for you when it's good, and we can enjoy a weekend every now and then until the mission is complete, OK?"

"No, it's *not* OK. I understand, though. I don't like it, but I do understand," Nola said, pouting.

"Awww, come give me a kiss, baby," Hot Shot said smiling, relieved that she went with what he suggested without giving him hell. Everything was falling in place. Now, all he had to do was find Franco and end his life, and then all will be well. *Come outside, Franco. Stop hiding from me,* Hot Shot said to himself.

Chapter Twenty-eight

Hot Shot was following Cotton to the Tams so he could meet with Piru Pete. When Cotton pulled into the parking lot of Tams, Hot Shot went across the street, parked in the Louisiana Chicken restaurant parking lot, and waited for Piru Pete to arrive. Ten minutes later, Piru Pete pulled into the restaurant's parking lot. He got out of the car, followed by another tall, dark-skinned man. Hot Shot sat up in his seat to get a better look at this new man Piru Pete put into their business. The two men went inside and met Cotton. A few minutes later, Cotton texted Hot Shot, letting him know the money was on point. Hot Shot texted Cotton back, telling him he could leave. He then texted Piru Pete and told him to head to the Food For Less so that they could make the exchange for the weapons. Hot Shot watched as the three men made their exit from Tams.

As Hot Shot was about to pull out of the restaurant, he noticed two men come from the other side of Tams with guns in their hands. They ran up on Cotton. Hot Shot knew it was a robbery. So he turned on to Central, and once he crossed Rosecrans, he made a right turn and came into the parking lot of Tams, the same side where the robbers had come from. Hot Shot ran up on the robbers coming from the front, thinking their robbery was successful.

Wrong. Neither of the robbers saw Hot Shot . . . until it was too late.

Hot Shot punched the robber holding the duffel bag of money, knocking him out cold. The other robber raised his pistol when Hot Shot whacked him with his gun, dazing him, but he didn't fall, so Hot Shot hit him again. This time, the robber fell to the ground, unconscious. Hot Shot returned to his car and called Cotton, who had called him several times.

"Boss man, it was a fucking setup! They got the money. Don't give that fool nothing."

Hot Shot smiled and said, "No, they didn't. Everything is all good. I got all the money now, so don't worry. Go back to the house."

"Are you sure?"

"Yes, I got it from here," Hot Shot in a determined voice.

He then called Piru Pete. When Pete answered the phone, Hot Shot said, "You know you're playing with your life, right?"

"On Piru, that wasn't on me. I didn't know about that grimy shit. It was all on CK Bone, not me."

"Is CK Bone the tall, dark-skinned fool with you?"

"Yeah, on Piru."

"Give him the phone."

Piru Pete gave his phone to the other man. Hot Shot said, "You're playing a dangerous game. I want to thank you for the donation because this money now belongs to me. If you want to play games, then we'll play."

"Man, that wasn't on me. Those niggas must have been watching us."

Hot Shot hung up the phone and slowly drove through the Tams parking lot, shaking his head as he passed Piru Pete and the other man. As he headed home, he thought that it might be jacking season. This was the second time someone had tried to rob his people in two days. Unfortunately, there were some thirsty men out here in

California. "It's time to go before I kill someone out here," Hot Shot muttered.

When he made it home, he was in the middle of the story when Cotton entered the house, looking like he was ready to kill someone.

"I'm telling you, Boss man, we need to get out of Cali because these fools will make me hurt somebody."

When she heard Cotton's voice, Lola came out of their bedroom and stood by Cotton's side, trying to find out what had happened.

"Yes, it seems like they think we're soft. So we need to find those dudes and pull up, letting them know we want all the smoke."

"You already know I'm with that."

"Say less."

Nola sat there staring at Cotton and Hot Shot, completely lost. "Will you finish telling me what happened?"

"Oh, my bad, baby." Hot Shot apologized and went on and told her what had happened at Tams. When he finished, he grabbed his phone and called JT.

"Man, I'm tired of this shit."

"What are you talking about, son?"

"These streets are getting crazy." He then told JT about the botched robbery.

"Yes, they are, son."

"In two days, people have tried to rob us twice. I'm so ready to get out of here. I'm going to end up killing these thirsty men. It's time to go, JT."

"I'm on it. Give me a few days. Try not to do something you'll regret. I'll get at the director and see if he's figured out what state you will visit next. In the meantime, I need you to remain calm and *think* before you let your temper get the best of you."

"I hear you, JT. I don't know if Piru Pete set that up or if he's telling me the truth, but either way, I'm done with him. This mission is complete. It's time to hit the road."

"I'm on it," JT said again and ended the call.

"I'm about to go calm down. Be ready to roll in thirty minutes or so," Hot Shot told Cotton as he headed to his bedroom, followed by Nola.

When they were gone, Lola asked Cotton a question. "Who is JT, baby? Why does Shot have to call him? JT's the plug?"

"Yeah, JT is the plug."

"Have you ever met him?"

"Yeah, a couple of times."

"He gotta be major to be able to give Shot everything he does. Guns, oxy, meth, coke, and weed."

"Right. JT is the man, baby. Period. There's nothing he can't get his hands on. That's why it's crucial for Shot not to make any mistakes. It may seem like he's extra with it, but he's making sure everything stays good so that he won't lose the plug," Cotton lied.

"I understand."

"Let me get ready because when Shot is on one, it gets ugly." "What y'all about to go do, baby?"

"Turn up. Time to spank those fools. Gotta let them fools know that they can't get at us like we some chumps."

"Be careful, baby."

Cotton smiled and said, "Say less."

Chapter Twenty-nine

Hot Shot came down the stairs dressed in black camouflage pants with a black hoodie. Cotton was waiting for him in the living room, dressed identically. No words were spoken as they left the house. Once inside the truck, they checked and rechecked their weapons, attached silencers to their pistols, and were off. As they headed toward the city of Compton, Hot Shot pulled out his phone and called Piru Pete.

"What's up, Pete?"
"Look, P, you got this shit all wrong. The homie says he had nothing to do with that shit."
"I disagree. He's lying. How would they know where to be to make the move they made against you?"
"I dunno, P. For real, I don't. CK Bone ain't like that, though. He's serious when it comes to business. He's reputable in these Bompton streets, and his name means everything to him. He doesn't need a jacket like that. Jacking fools ain't his get down, P."
"If he didn't have anything to do with that shit, then the only other person who would have been able to make that happen was you, Pete. So . . . Who is it? You or CK Bone?"
"Now, you know damn well it wasn't me, P. That wouldn't make any sense."
"Actually, it makes a lot of sense because it gives you the advantage and a perfect alibi like you just gave. The more I think about it, I know it was you, wasn't it, Pete?"

"Fuck no. I swear, man, I didn't have shit to do with that mess, P."

"OK, then I need to know where CK Bone is."

"He's in his hood, most likely."

"What hood?"

"Fruit Town Piru."

"If I'm not able to touch him up, you make sure you tell him that his actions caused this reaction," Hot Shot said and ended the call.

He drove toward the Fruit Town Piru neighborhood. They didn't see anyone hanging out, so Hot Shot turned on Rosecrans Avenue and went toward Gonzalez Park, a well-known hangout for the FTPs. As he drove by the park, he saw several FTPs in the area. So he went farther down Rosecrans, made a U-turn, and parked the car across the street from Gonzalez Park. Cotton followed Hot Shot as they crossed the street and entered the park.

As they strolled casually into the area, Hot Shot spotted CK Bone amongst a small pack of Pirus. As they got closer to the Pirus, CK Bone looked up, saw the two men, noticed Cotton, and instantly started running. Both Hot Shot and Cotton began to fire their guns at the Pirus. They hit a few closest to them, but Hot Shot had CK Bones in his sight, and he wasn't going to get away from him. He ran hard past the fallen Pirus on the ground and got close enough to get a good shot off at CK Bone, who was trying to get inside his car. Hot Shot let off two more rounds and caught CK Bone in the legs. CK Bone fell to the ground, and Hot Shot ran up to him and wasted no time. He shot CK Bone twice in the head, turned, and sprinted through the park with Cotton right behind him. They returned to the car and sped away from Compton, leaving a bloody park full of wounded and dead Pirus.

***

Cotton and Lola were having drinks and chilling, enjoying themselves, when he got a call from Yolanda. He sent the call to voicemail, but Yolanda kept calling back, so he told Lola he had to take this call from her. She smiled and told him to go ahead.

"What's good, Yolanda?"

"What's with the sending me straight to voicemail shit? So *that's* how you do me, Cotton?"

"I'm kinda busy right now. What's up?"

"I need your help. My brother's house got raided this morning, and they took his money. He needs you to help him with bail money."

"That's crazy. Did they get anything else?"

"Yep. A lot of pills."

"Damn. How much is his bail?"

"A hundred thousand. Ten bands with property."

"I don't own any property to help out."

"My mother will put up her house. We just need the cash."

"Ten bands is a lot for me right now, Yolanda. Let me make a call to see if my people can help me out. I'll hit you back."

"Please, Cotton, we really need to get him out."

"I'll do what I can. But like I said, let me get at my people to see what they can help me with. We've done some good business with Hakeem, so my people should look out."

"OK. Call me and let me know because I'll go get a payday loan and see what I can get. I want my brother out of there."

"Say less," Cotton said and ended the call. He proceeded to call Hot Shot and let him know what happened with Hakeem. He had to play it off with Lola right in front of him. She couldn't know that Hakeem's arrest was because Cotton had it set up. Hot Shot made sure that it was understood that he didn't want Lola to know the business about him being an undercover FBI agent, so he had to have this mock conversation with Hot Shot purely to keep Lola out of the business.

"What up, Boss man?"

"Nothing much. What's good with you?" asked Hot Shot.

"Having lunch with Lola. Just got a call, my boy, Hakeem, got knocked this morning, and his sister needs help raising the bail money. I told her I don't have the ten bands she needs, but I'd check with you to see if you could help her get her brother out of jail."

"You're getting at me about this because Lola is with you?"

"Facts."

"Very good. I just paid JT, and my funds are tight right now. Will your boy make good on giving the money back because it's a loan, not a favor?"

"Well, she said they took all his money when they hit his spot. So most likely, he's going to want me to give him some consignment and try to make good like that."

"I don't know, then. You know how I feel about the front thing. When you get home, we'll look at it."

"OK. I'll be there in about an hour or so."

"See you then," Hot Shot said as he ended their fake conversation. He was glad Cotton was keeping Lola in the blind about what he does. Nola stressed that there was no way Lola could ever find out about him being an FBI agent. She would flip out and be extremely upset about how he was responsible for putting her brother and cousins in jail. So he had to make sure Cotton did not tell Lola their secret.

When Cotton set his phone down, Lola asked him if they would bail out Hakeem.

Cotton shrugged and said, "I don't know, baby. I mean, I got the ten bands, but that will be touching my vault, and I only hit the vault for emergencies."

"What did Shot say?"

"He's going to think about it, but he wasn't feeling it when I told him Hakeem will most likely want some consignment to get back on his feet. He doesn't like to front no one who ain't on the team."

"I see. Old boy should've known better not to shit where he eats. I mean, he had drugs *and* his money together in his house where he rests his head. Not smart at all."

"Right."

"If you guys get him out, you still must wonder if he's solid. He could get bailed out, then set you up to make his case disappear. Or he could be a stand-up dude and just need your help to compensate for his losses. Or y'all could leave him in there and wonder if he'll snitch. That's a catch-22 for real, baby."

"You're right. I'll let Boss man make the decision. Right now, I'm trying to finish enjoying my lunch with my girl."

That made Lola smile as she leaned over and kissed her man for saying such sweet words. *Guess I am built for this relationship shit,* she said to herself as she got back to eating her salad.

Chapter Thirty

Fabian was waiting in the holding cell at the Long Beach Police Station after being processed into the jail's system. He couldn't believe his luck—first, the botched attempted robbery on Lola. Second, getting beaten damn near to death by Nola and her people and losing all his money. And last, his house was raided, and he was arrested for possessing methamphetamine. *How in the fuck am I going to get out of this shit?* he wondered as he waited for the detectives to talk to him. He had no problem snitching. He wasn't built for no jail time. So he asked to speak with a detective in hopes he could give them enough information to get out of this mess. The problem was that he didn't have much to tell the police. All he knew was Lola's name and phone number. He could give up some of the other people he used to deal with before he met Lola. But they were low-level types, and he was sure that wouldn't impress the detectives enough to let him get out. Damn.

Hot Shot was sitting on the opposite side of JT's desk and listened to JT give him the details of his next mission. *Looks like Cotton and I are on our way back to Texas. Houston is the city this time. Cotton will love that. Houston is a four-and-a-half hour drive from Dallas, and I'm sure Cotton would love to visit his family while we're in Houston,* Hot Shot said to himself. *Nola will certainly want to come on this mission for the same reason Cotton will.*

"You see, son, the Crips and Bloods are heavy out there in Houston, and the director wants to take as many of them down as possible. Their drug of choice is that cocaine. They move a lot of cocaine, mostly in Louisiana. Some heavy players are in Houston. They're really flashy, so we're setting you up with a downtown condo as well as a flashy car and jewels."

"Jewels? You know I don't need no jewels, JT."

"You will with this mission; trust me. We have a CI that will take you to where you will solidify your cover. The CI will also show you who the main targets are. Any questions?"

"No."

"Good. We're still getting things in place. Everything should be ready in about a week or so."

"I'll be ready."

"You did real good out here, son. Finally, we put a dent in the I-13s. The Fabian character and Hakeem were also good takedowns. We gotta keep it up. The more good you do, the better."

"Right."

"I wanna also commend you on not going crazy with the Mexicans. That was a pleasant surprise."

Hot Shot smiled and said, "You ordered me to stand down, so I followed my orders."

"Since when?"

"This mission."

"The first time I can remember you following any damn orders. Regardless, I'm glad you did this time. I know how hard that was for you. That's another reason why I'm getting you outta California. I don't want you to lose it going after those guys."

"I'm good," lied Hot Shot.

"Alrighty, then, that's about it. I'll get with you and let you know when you can get to Houston."

Hot Shot stood, shook hands with JT, and headed back home so he could have a sit-down with the team. He was ready to get out of California, but he still had to get his hands on Franco. He didn't want to leave until he got that murdering bastard. He had a week or so to find him and prayed he would. If not, he would have to wait, and waiting for Franco's death would continue to mess his head up more than it already was. He had to be totally focused when he was on a mission. He couldn't afford to have his head all over the place while on assignment. Mistakes could happen, and he couldn't allow that. It would put Cotton in danger as well as himself.

"Where are you, Franco? Come out of hiding, you coward. Come out, so I can take your life," Hot Shot said as he pulled into the driveway of his home.

As soon as he walked into the house, he heard Cotton and Lola arguing.

"I don't give a damn what you're talking about. You don't need to be going out to no damn club. What if you bump into that fool Fabian or some shit? Fall back and let that go, Lola, for real now," said Cotton.

Lola was about to say something slick when she saw Hot Shot enter the house, so she decided not to.

"If you don't want me to go for safety reasons, then come with me. Or come watch my back while I have some fun. I'm about done with the tourist shit. It's like I've been out here all my life. I know my way around Sunny Southern California now. So it's time to go kick it. You know how we do in Texas, baby."

"Right, but this ain't Texas, Lola."

"I hear you, baby."

"Looks like you lovebirds have things figured out."

Cotton rolled his eyes.

Lola laughed.

Nola came downstairs, saw everyone, and joined them in the living room.

"Since we're all here, I have some news about our new get-down. We headed back to Texas."

"What? When?" asked Cotton.

"As soon as JT gets everything in place."

"Where in Texas?" asked Nola.

"Houston."

"*That's* what's up. That's only a four-hour drive to Dallas. So we can go home and spend some time out there, Nola," said Lola.

Nola was staring at Hot Shot as she responded to her sister. "We're not invited, sister. We can still go back home for a while, though, while Hot Shot and Cotton do their thing in Houston."

"The fuck! *You* may not be invited, but I damn sure will be in Houston if this black-ass man is there. If you think I'm going to let his loose dick ass run wild in Houston, you got another think coming," Lola said, glaring at Cotton, *daring* him to go against her.

Before Cotton could speak, Hot Shot said, "Lola, when I go outta town for business, that's what it is: business. Y'all will be able to come to Houston for sure. As far as staying down there with us, that cannot happen. We need to be totally focused on getting the money—no distractions. As much as I love my wife and hate being away from her, it is what it is. You two going to Dallas would be a good thing. You won't be too far, so coming to Houston for a weekend wouldn't be a problem."

"I hear you, Shot, but you cannot speak on Mister Dick Slanger. This man will be on every stank bitch in Houston."

Cotton laughed.

"You're right. I can't speak on him. But I can speak on how my business will be conducted. No distractions, Lola."

Lola stared at Cotton with a look that made him cringe. He remained silent, hoping Shot would be able to handle this situation.

"It's all good, sister. We'll be able to go back home and have a good time. While they're in Houston doing them, we'll be in Dallas doing us," Nola said with a smile on her face.

Smiling now, Lola said, "You're sure right. Plus, when we do go to Houston, we can go see brother."

"*You* can go see him, but I won't be able to. Remember, I'm a convicted felon."

"Girl, you're not thinking. I go up to see Troy using your name. So on a Saturday, I'll drive up there to see him as you. Then on Sunday's visit, you can go see him as you."

Nola smiled. "You're right, sister."

"Good. It's all good then," Hot Shot said as he went upstairs, followed by Nola. He hoped and prayed that she wasn't about to give him the business.

As soon as they were upstairs, Lola went off on her man.

"If you think you're going to be out there in Houston fucking everything, I'm going to bite your fucking dick off, Cotton. I'm not fucking playing with your ass."

"I don't see why you're tripping, baby. I thought you said we would have an open relationship. As long as I let you know what's up, it was supposed to be all good."

"Yeah, I said that shit, but fuck that. I gotta be close to you so you won't get *too* stupid with it."

"I'm going to be focused on the business more than I will a bitch out there. And if I do, I will make sure that I keep it a hunnid with you and let you know about it, baby. So, ease up. It's all good. We all good. You're boo, and no one can knock you out of the number one spot, baby." He gave her a hug and a kiss and smiled.

Cotton couldn't wait to get to Houston. Houston had some of the baddest bitches, and he would love it. He was smiling as he hugged his woman.

Houston, here we come.

Chapter Thirty-one

Fabian was in his den, sitting at his desk, happy as hell to be a free man. He was able to give the narcotics detectives enough information to get a get-out-of-jail-free card as long as he delivered. He was about to set up drug dealers by purchasing drugs from them. Meth, pills, PCP—whatever. He would then give the information to the police and let the detectives do their thing. He wished he could give them that bitch Lola. He will never forget how she and her people did him. "I'd love to get that bitch caught the fuck up," he said. His life was so good until he let his cousins talk him into letting them try to rob her. And what did he get for doing that? Lost damn near all his money, got beat damn near to death, his cousins ended up shot, and then went to jail for possession of firearms, and last, his house got raided, and he went to jail. Now, he had to be a snitch and set up people just to remain free without a drug case. *God doesn't like ugly,* he thought.

After getting dressed, he grabbed his keys, left his house, and headed to the Melody Bar. He wore his dark shades to hide the bruises around his eyes. He needed to get drunk. He didn't want to get drunk at home alone, so he thought going to the Melody Bar to knock down a few drinks while listening to some good music would put him in a better mood.

Lola and Nola entered the Melody looking so good that every male they walked by spoke, whistled, or said something corny. They laughed as they went to the bar outside of the club. After getting their drinks, they found an empty table and sat down, bobbing their heads to the music. They were having a good time, even though Cotton acted like a jerk. Even if Fabian was at the club, what could he do to them inside the club? Nothing. Lola shook those thoughts off and sipped her drink.

Nola was enjoying her drink, thinking about how she didn't like her husband going to Houston without her. She knew it was a work-related job and all, but still, she should be allowed to go with him. *I should be going with him if we're a team like he said. It's not like I'm going to interfere with the mission. We'll have to talk about that shit some more,* she said to herself. She wasn't trying to mess up her mood. She came out with her sister to have a good time, which she intended to do.

The night was getting cool. Lola was dancing in front of their table while Nola laughed at her. They were on their third drink and feeling no pain. However, all of their fun came to a screeching halt when Nola saw Fabian come out on the patio.

Fuck.

Nola quickly texted Hot Shot and told him that Fabian was in the club, but he hadn't seen them. Yet. Hot Shot texted her right back, saying he was on his way. Nola breathed a sigh of relief. If something was going to pop off, she knew it would be all good when her husband and Cotton got there.

"Lola, come sit down for a minute," Nola told her sister as she kept her eyes on Fabian as he moved around the patio, stopping to shake a few different guys' hands.

"What's wrong, sister? You got that funny look on your face when you're nervous," Lola said as she sat next to Nola.

"First, you need to prepare for one hell of 'I told you so' lecture from Cotton."

"What the hell are you talking about, sister? I ain't worried about Cotton's paranoid ass."

"Second, Fabian is here."

"Gurl, you lying."

"Nope. Turn your head slightly to the right and see for yourself."

Lola turned and saw Fabian talking to some females. Then she turned back to her sister with an evil look in her eyes.

Shaking her head, Nola said, "Calm down, Lola. Don't do no stupid shit. Shot and Cotton are on their way."

"What? Why you call them, Nola? That fuck boy ain't gon' do nothing to us in the damn club. Now, Cotton gon' come in this bitch being extra as fuck. Damn, you tripped the fuck out by calling them. What, you scared of that bitch? I ain't. I should go over there and slap the shit out of his ass."

"No, you shouldn't. Calm down. I called Shot because we don't know what might happen when we leave the club. I agree. I don't think Fabian would do shit to us here, but what about when we walk out? I ain't taking no chances."

"Fuck that shit. That coward ain't trying to fuck with us."

"You can't say that shit for certain. We beat the fuck out of that man and took his money. You cannot be absolutely sure he won't trip the fuck out when he sees us. He's a fuck boy, for sure, but he's still a man. We're females, and he has the advantage, even though it will be two against one. I *had* to call Shot. So, relax, and let's see how it goes."

Lola was seething mad. She wanted to confront Fabian, but her sister's logic gave her pause. Instead, she smiled as she thought about how it would be when Cotton and Hot Shot arrived. She was going to act up for real, then.

Nola noticed the devious look on her sister's face and said, "And don't you be on the bullshit when Shot and Cotton get here. I see that look on your face."

Lola laughed and said, "I hate that you know me so damn well. I'm trying to have a good time. Why in the fuck would that bitch Fabian choose tonight to come to the damn club? Ugh."

"We should have gone to the Nile Bar instead."

"That place is cool but not as cool as it is here. Look at that bitch, Fabian. I bet he's wearing those dark shades to hide them black eyes we gave his ass," Lola said, laughing.

"I know, right? Come on. Let's go to the bathroom real quick."

"You go on. I'm good. I'm going to the bar to get another drink. Do you want one?"

"Lola, come with me. I gotta use it. Then we'll go to the bar together. We shouldn't split up."

"Would you go on and take your scary ass to the bathroom before you pee on yourself? I'm good. We are good. Damn, you acting real weak right now," Lola said as she stood and went to the bar.

Nola went to the bathroom and handled her business as quickly as possible. When she returned to her seat, she saw Lola at the bar talking to some big guy who looked like one of those huge football player types. She sighed with relief when she saw that Fabian was still conversing with some females at the back of the patio.

"Where the hell are you, Shot?" she said quietly.

As if on cue, Hot Shot and Cotton came out to the patio. Hot Shot saw Nola and headed straight toward her, followed by Cotton. Both of their faces looked like they were ready to hurt someone.

"Oh shit," she said to herself.

"You okay?" Hot Shot asked as he scanned the patio until he spotted Fabian talking to some females.

Lola came to the table, wrapped her arms around Cotton, and said, "Don't start. Everything is good. Nola's scary ass called y'all. That fool hasn't said one word to us."

"I told you, but you refused to listen. You would think you would get it. Damn, baby," Cotton said as he too spotted Fabian.

"No need to get extra, baby. It's all good."

"I still feel like going and socking the shit out of that bitch."

"I do too. But that would be overkill for real. So let that fuck boy be, baby."

"OK. We might as well get on out of here," Hot Shot said as he continued to stare at Fabian.

"No fucking way. I'm not letting that fool ruin my night out. Y'all better get a drink and come sit down with us."

Hot Shot knew better but went on and sat down while Cotton and Lola went to the bar to get something to drink. Nola saw the look on her husband's face and knew he wanted to leave.

"One drink, and we can get out of here, baby. Lola has to prove her point. She's always been that way."

"That's not good, baby."

"I know."

"I know you're not feeling the Houston thing. Honestly, I'm not either, but it has to be that way until I feel it's cool for you to join me. Please don't trip. You know I got you, and I never want to be away from you for too long."

"That makes me feel better. So I'm cool with that," she said and kissed her husband. "You know that gets you some good loving when we get home."

"Is that right?"

"Yep."

"Mmmm, I can go for that."

Cotton and Lola returned with their drinks and sat down. Hot Shot watched Fabian as he headed in their

direction. Fabian paused as he passed their table. When
he recognized who was sitting there, he turned around,
speed-walked to the back exit, and got the hell out of the
club. They all started laughing.

"See, I told you that bitch-ass fuck boy don't want no
smoke," Lola said, still laughing.

Nola was relieved, and so was Cotton. Lola was highly
amused. Hot Shot was horny and ready to leave. He was
thinking about the hot sex his wife had promised him. He
was *more* than ready to go.

Chapter Thirty-two

Fabian couldn't believe his luck. He heard Lola and her people laughing at him as he exited the club. Yeah, he would be the last one to laugh, Fabian said to himself as he got into his car and cruised around the parking lot until he saw the black Audi that Lola drove every time they met. He parked his car in the cut and waited patiently until he saw Lola, her sister, and the two guys that came into his place and beat his ass. He had the urge to pull up on them and start shooting. But instead, he laughed again and watched as the group got into their cars and left the club's parking lot.

He followed them for fifteen minutes until they pulled into the driveway of a nice home in Culver City. He put the address into his phone and went back to the club to finish drinking and enjoying himself. Tonight was a good night, after all. He couldn't wait to call the detectives and tell them where Lola lived, and he was certain drugs were on the premises. He thought back to how Lola bragged how her people had whatever drugs he wanted and guns too.

"Yeah, bitch, you and your people are going to jail. Laugh at *that*," he said gleefully.

Hot Shot woke up the next morning feeling good as he went downstairs and woke Cotton so they could do their morning workout. He was in a good mood because his wife treated him *really* nice by sexing him crazy. He couldn't believe how turned on he got whenever they made love. His wife was the best, and their lovemaking was out of this world. After they finished working out, he went and showered. He was getting dressed when Nola opened her eyes and smiled.

"Damn, Shot, you put it on me last night, baby," she said as she stretched and let the sheets slide off her body, revealing her perfect D-cups.

Hot Shot groaned and said, "*I* put it on you? No, baby, *you* put it on *me,* especially when you did that freaky thang with your mouth. You know that drives me nuts."

"It does, huh? OK, come here and let me put it on you some more and drive you nuts again."

"Tempting as that sounds, I have some business to take care of."

Pouting and grabbing both of her breasts, using her thumbs and forefingers to play with each nipple, she asked, "Are you *sure,* baby? I promise it won't take me long to get a good nut out of your sexy ass."

His mouth was watering, and his dick was getting so hard as he watched his wife playing with her nipples. "I guess I can be a little late," he said as he stripped and joined his wife on the bed.

Nola grabbed his hard dick and moaned as she stroked it. She then put it in her mouth and began sucking it slowly while she let her tongue ring work its magic across his dickhead. She seductively licked his dick. Finally, Hot Shot couldn't take it any longer, so he pulled her off his dick, and she eased on top of him. He inserted his hard dick inside of her hot, wet pussy. She couldn't stop herself from screaming how good he felt inside her. She was riding him fast and hard until they came together, totally enraptured in sexual bliss.

It took them a few minutes to get their breathing back to normal. Then finally, they got out of bed and took a shower together. Hot Shot dressed again while Nola wore a pair of shorts and a tee. Afterward, they went downstairs to see Lola and Cotton sitting on the couch watching the news.

"Damn, gurl, you sure were loud up there. We had to turn the damn TV up to drown out all that damn screaming your ass was doing," Lola said, laughing.

Nola flipped the bird at her, smiling.

"Yeah, Boss man, it sounded as if you were getting *your* scream on too," added Cotton, joining Lola's laughter.

"It's obvious that you two are sexed out with each other if you're down here listening to what my wife and I are doing in our bedroom. So ya can't watch porn to help you get your groove back on?" Hot Shot said, grinning as he went into the kitchen. He grabbed a bottle of water and an apple, then went back into the living room.

"Just so you know, there's absolutely *nothing* wrong with our sex. It's fire as ever. Cotton is a true Texas stud, believe that, Mr. Shot," Lola said and laughed.

"Facts," added Cotton.

Hot Shot and Nola laughed and, in unison, said, "TMI." Then they all started laughing.

Hot Shot stopped laughing when his phone started ringing. He saw Toker's name on the call and silently prayed that he had some news on Franco's whereabouts.

"What up, Toker?"

"Franco's back, and he told me to get at you. He wants ten AR-15s and ten AK-47s ASAP."

"OK. Let me make the call, and I'll hit you back. It most likely will take a day or two."

"Say less," Toker said and ended the call.

"Franco's back in play. Time to end that fool."

"Good," said Cotton. "Let's finish this shit right out here."

"Exactly," said Hot Shot.

"I'm glad. Make sure you make that fucking Mexican feel the pain and know why he's being served," said Nola.

"Right," said Cotton.

"OK, who is this Franco, and why you gotta dead him?" Lola asked.

"I'll explain later, sister," said Nola.

Hot Shot walked out of the house with his phone to his ear, telling JT he was on his way over to talk to him. He got inside his car feeling good because there would be no more stalling. He would finally be able to get his revenge for the murders of his family.

When he made it to JT's house and told him about the gun order for the I-13s, he tried to keep his normally calm demeanor and hide his excitement. However, his former sergeant in the Special Forces unit of the United States Army knew Hot Shot too well and wasn't falling for his act. So to make sure his hunch was correct that Hot Shot had something "extra" planned, JT set him up.

"We don't need to fill that order. We've done enough damage to the I-13s. The director is ready for us to move on so we can get everything set up for you in Houston."

Hot Shot knew JT just as well as JT knew him, so with his poker face intact, he told JT, "I'm feeling that. One last move on the Mexicans puts the hurt to them to real decent. I'm sure the director won't mind if we got at them one last time. More arrests mean more of those slimeballs are off the streets of Inglewood."

OK, I see you trying to be real smooth, Hot Shot, JT said to himself. "Cut the bullshit, son, and talk to me. You and I know you have something extra going on behind this next takedown. Be real with me, and I won't dead it. You try me with that poker face if you want, and you'll be on the first plane I can get booked for Houston."

"Franco went off the radar, and I was going to accept it and let it go until I could get back here and deal with it. Whether it happens now or later, it's definitely happening, JT. Franco is not one of the men who killed my family, but he's the man who gave the green light for it to happen. For that, he has to die by my hand. No games."

JT nodded and said, "I know I won't be able to stop you. And the director wants you to end this. He's worried the hate you have for those Mexicans could derail your focus and mess up what we got going on. Can you handle this and bounce back, son?"

"Yes, I can, JT."

"How will you do it?"

"After we make this last deal, and when they get raided, I'll handle it."

"You sure?"

"I've never been more sure of anything in my life."

"Get the job done, son. We got a lot of work to do."

"Understood."

Hot Shot left JT's house, and as he pulled into his driveway, he noticed a black Camry with dark tint parked three houses down from his home. It screamed "Police" to him. It may not stand out to an average person, but it certainly stood out to Hot Shot. He wondered how and why they would be watching him. How in the hell would they even know where he stayed? These questions were swirling in his head as he walked into his house.

He went to his bedroom and grabbed his badge. He was glad everyone was gone, especially Lola. That way, he could handle this without her finding out he was a federal agent. He came back outside and made sure that the black Camry was still there. It was. He walked toward the car. While standing on the sidewalk next to the Camry, the police officer inside rolled down his window and smiled.

"Can I help you, young man?"

"Yes, you can. I have a few questions."

"About what?"

Hot Shot could see it was a white-and-Black undercover team. So he smiled and said, "I need to know why you two are watching my place."

"Why would we be watching your house?"

Hot Shot laughed and said, "Standard stakeout procedures, Officer. Three to four houses away from the target."

The Black officer sitting in the driver's seat leaned over his partner and said, "You sound like a police officer."

"No, I'm not a police officer. I'm a federal undercover agent," Hot Shot said as he pulled out his badge and gave it to the white officer.

Both of the police officers started laughing.

"We are sorry, Agent Gaines. We got a CI who told us that your house could have some guns and drugs."

"Really?"

"Yeah, we raided his house last week and caught him slipping with a nice amount of meth. He sang like a bird before we got him to the station. He claimed he mainly dealt with this female with a twin sister. He didn't know where she stayed at first. So we agreed to let him out to get us anything he could get. Then he called us this morning with this address, claiming this twin lives there, and she bragged to him how she could get him any drug he wanted and guns. So we thought we'd come to sit on the house to see if we could learn anything about this twin he told us about."

Hot Shot smiled and said, "This CI's name is Fabian, correct?"

"Exactly."

"My office is why you guys got the tip to get him. We thought he was heavy in the game. Once we found out he was in the minor leagues, my boss gave him to you guys. Lola, the twin, is who we used to get his attention."

Both the narcotic detectives started laughing.

"OK, fellas, I won't hold you up. I'm sure you'll make sure that Fabian gets to work somewhere else."

"Exactly. Take it easy, Gaines," said the white officer. The Black detective started the car, and they eased away from the curb.

Hot Shot went inside the house and told Nola and Cotton what had happened when they returned.

"That bitch-ass clown is a fucking snitch now. That's funny," said Cotton. "Yeah, it is, but you know what's *not* funny?" said Nola.

"What?" asked Cotton.

"That snitch knows where we live. That means we were slipping last night when we left the club."

"You're right, baby. It's things like that that cannot happen. We were so amped that we didn't watch our six as we should have. We thought Fabian ran from us. But instead, he went and got in the cut, waited for us to leave, and followed us home."

"You think he needs to be handled, Boss man?"

Hot Shot had a frown on his face as he contemplated if they should kill Fabian. Then after a minute or so, he shook his head. "Nah, he's too caught up trying to set up fools for the locals. He won't be a threat. Still, watch your back when you move. I'm about to handle Franco, and then we're out. Franco is all that matters now."

"Facts," said Cotton.

"Indeed," said Nola.

Chapter Thirty-three

Hot Shot had the guns loaded in the back of his SUV, and he was waiting for Toker to call him so he could let him know where he would meet Cotton to make sure the money was right as usual. He decided to have Franco meet him at the Morningside High School parking lot, where they had previously met. Hot Shot would go to Franco's house after the exchange and wait for Franco to get home. He would have Cotton handle Franco's two homeboys and do Franco right there. The thought of kidnapping Franco and taking him somewhere was out the window. Too risky. This wasn't a movie. This was real life, and Hot Shot wasn't taking any chances. Franco was dying in a few hours.

Toker called, and Hot Shot told him that Cotton would meet him at Brolly Hut Hamburger stand on 112th Street and Crenshaw.

"When Cotton calls me and tells me the money is right, tell Franco to meet me at the same place we met before, and we'll handle up."

"Say less. I'm headed to Brolly Hut now," said Toker.

"OK, Cotton will be there in about fifteen minutes."

"Cool," Toker said and ended the call.

"All right, let's do this."

"You sure you don't need me, baby?" asked Nola.

"Nah. We got this, baby. It'll be over tonight. Love you."

"Love you more, Shot. Be careful."

He smiled and said, "Always."

Cotton smiled and said, "See how much love your sister shows that man? Why can't I get that kinda love, Lola? Unfortunately, all I get is that bomb sex."

"Exactly. So go handle your business and come back and get more of this bomb sex," she said, smiling. Then she went to her man and gave him a soft kiss. "Be careful, baby."

"Say less," Cotton said and walked out of the house behind Hot Shot.

Fifteen minutes later, Cotton pulled into the parking lot of Brolly Hut and saw Toker's car. He got out of his truck, got inside the car, and said, "What's good, Toker?"

"The same old thing, homie." Toker gave Cotton a small duffel bag and watched as Cotton started counting the money.

"Looks like we are all good here."

"You know it's all good, homie," Toker said . . . then pulled out a pistol and aimed it at Cotton's head. Then he said, "Make the call to let your boy know it's all good, or you die."

"Are you sure you want to do this shit, Toker?"

"I don't have a choice. Franco knows the truth. He went to Mexico and met some crazy witch bitch he believes in, and she told him some form of police had set him up. He was going to kill my entire family if I didn't fess up. He gave me his word that he wouldn't hurt me if I did this, so I had no choice. Make the fucking call, Cotton, man. I don't want to kill you, but I will. Franco thinks I'm a fool. No way in hell would he ever let me make it. He's going to kill me anyway. But I got something for his ass. That money will be enough to get me and mine up outta Cali."

"Don't be stupid, dog. You know all we gotta do is call our people and have everyone picked up. No one has to die today, Toker."

Shaking his head, Toker said, "Nah, bro, it has to go down like this. Make. The. Fucking. Call. Now. Cotton. I ain't telling you again."

Cotton's mind was racing. He didn't know what to do, but he knew he had to warn Hot Shot, or he was as good as dead. So he pulled out his phone and silently prayed Hot Shot caught the signal he was about to give him.

Hot Shot was standing outside his SUV talking to Franco as they waited for the call from Cotton. He noticed that Franco brought three of his goons this time instead of two like the last time they met to handle business. *Guess he's paranoid,* Hot Shot thought as he waited for the call from Cotton. Finally, his phone started ringing, and he saw it was Cotton.

"What's up? We good?"

"Yeah, we Gucci. Nola and Lola are on the way to you," said Cotton praying that Hot Shot would instantly know something was wrong.

Hot Shot did, in fact, get the warning and now had to stall for a few seconds to send a distress call to Nola.

"OK, cool," he said and walked to the back of the SUV so he could open the door so Franco's goons could start transferring the guns into their SUV. Hot Shot then called Nola but didn't say anything to her. He was standing on the side of his SUV and watched as the Mexicans unloaded his truck. He knew they were going to make a move because as soon as he got close to the door of his SUV, Franco came to stand next to him. Hot Shot acted like he was checking his phone and sent a quick text to Nola.

Follow me! Call JT.

She texted right back. OK.

He felt a little better, but his mind was all over the place. He took calming breaths and waited for the Mexicans to make their move. Being trained in hand-to-hand combat, he knew he could take on all of them, but they had weapons, and that's another story altogether. When they finished, he was ready.

"It looks like we're all good, homes. Now, I need to get at you about something," said Franco as he turned and faced Hot Shot, holding a gun. "Did you think I would continue to be a dumb Mexican?"

Hot Shot put his phone in his pocket and asked, "What are you talking about? We've done good business. So what's the gun for?"

The three Mexican goons came from the other side of their SUV, and all had guns in their hands.

"When were you going to make your move on me, homes? Don't play dumb. Toker told me everything. You've been trying to get close to me so you could get your revenge on me for giving the order to have your family killed. So, when were you going to make your move, nigga?"

Hot Shot cringed and wanted to strike out but had no room to do so. "I was going to kill you later tonight when you went home to your house on Carson Street in Long Beach."

Franco smiled and said, "I respect that, nigga. You know you're dead, right? I should blast you right here and now, but I want to have some fun with you before I kill you, nigga. You see these two right here? They're the two that blew your father, mother, and brother's brains out. I'm going to let them torture you for a couple of hours, *then* blow your brains out. Get into your truck."

Hot Shot climbed into his SUV. Franco got into the passenger's seat, and two of the three Mexican goons got

in the backseat behind him. Franco ordered him to follow
the SUV with the guns. Hot Shot started his truck and did
as he was told. He wondered what Toker did to Cotton.
He hoped and prayed Nola heard what was said. He felt
a little better about his chances of making it out of this
mess because he knew for sure his wife had gotten his
text. *Come get me, baby,* he thought.

When Toker told Cotton to get out of his vehicle, Cotton just knew he was about to get shot in the back of the
head. So, he was shocked when he saw Toker back out of
the parking space and speed off down Crenshaw Boulevard. Cotton ran to his truck and tried to call Hot Shot,
and when he didn't get an answer, he knew it was all bad.
So, he called Nola, and she didn't answer either.

What the fuck? he screamed in his head. He called Lola,
and she yelled at him before he could even utter a word.

"Them Mexicans got Hot Shot, baby! We following Hot
Shot's locator to see where they're taking him."

"How do y'all know what happened?"

"Hot Shot called Nola and didn't say anything, and she
heard the Mexican tell Hot Shot how they about to take
him somewhere and torture him. But before that, he sent
Nola a text telling her to call JT. Where are you, baby? I
just knew you were somewhere dead. Oh my God, this is
so fucked up!"

"I'm good, baby. Toker set us up, but he let me go and
took off with the money. Where are y'all now?"

"I don't know. I'll put you on speaker and let Nola tell
you."

Once she was on speaker, Nola said, "We're driving
west on Century Boulevard, like headed toward LAX. The
locator keeps switching up, so that tells me they're driving. When they stop, then we'll know exactly where they
are. We gotta get there before they hurt Shot, Cotton."

"We will. Did you call JT?"

"Yes, he said he's following the guns, so once they stop, he too will know where they are."

"OK, good. I'm not far behind y'all, so keep at it, and I'll be with y'all in a li'l bit. I got an idea where they might be going."

"You better hurry up because as soon as they stop and the locator shows me where my man is, I'm going to get him."

"No. You are going to wait until I get there, Nola. Then we'll go in together."

"Well, you better hurry the fuck up because I ain't waiting too damn long. They got my fucking husband."

Cotton was shaking his head as he silently prayed nothing happened to Hot Shot. "Here we come, Boss man, here we come."

The End

Author's Note

OK, I got it going, didn't I? LOL. I hope my supporters have enjoyed this latest installment of my Hot Shot series. I had to let Hot Shot face the Mexicans that murdered his family. I hope everyone enjoyed the new twists I added with Lola and Cotton getting together. I swear I am having so much fun with this series. Should I stop? If Hot Shot dies, then how will I be able to keep it going? Who knows what my crazy mind will put together. I want everyone who buys my books to know I am forever grateful for your support. I'll do a stand-alone to give me a break on the Hot Shot series. Then I'll get right back at ya. Promise. I know everyone is waiting for *Gangsta Twist 4*. No worries. I will finish it this year as well. God bless you all. Thank you again so very much.

SPUD 6-22-22

Also Available

Carl Weber's:

Five Families of New York

Part 4: Queens

by

C. N. Phillips

Chapter 1

"Ahh!"

Lorenzo "Zo" Alverez's pained shout was probably heard throughout the property. He'd just stepped into the shower, and the moment the water hit his fair skin, he felt like he was on fire. He continued to curse under his breath as he adjusted the heat. The help was always turning the water heater up when he was least expecting it. In those moments, he understood what it must be like to be a lobster dropped in a boiling pot of doom.

Knock! Knock!

"You all right in there, shithead?" his younger sister Daniella's voice sounded from outside the door.

"I'm fine. They just adjusted the water heater again."

"Pussy."

"Whatever. Get out of my suite!" he shouted over his shoulder as he stepped into the shower again and slid the glass door closed.

He heard her say something else, but he couldn't make it out over the water. It was still steaming hot but bearable. He found himself wondering what Daniella was doing in his suite, especially when her suite was on the other side of the house. Probably snooping through his things again. Ever since their father, DeMarco Alverez, was killed by the Chinese, Daniella felt the need to double-check every business transaction that Zo finalized.

The Alverez family was one of five of the most dangerous and feared families in all of New York. They ran a foolproof weapons operation in Queens that brought in a lucrative exchange. Before Marco was killed, he was the head honcho, but the hat was inevitably tipped toward Zo. Had he been ready to take on the weight of carrying on his father's legacy? No. But he was trying.

With everything going on around him, Zo was forced to hit the ground running. At one point, the five most powerful families in New York worked together in harmony. A pact was drawn up before Zo was even born. The pact called for each family to have only one trade. That way no one would step on anyone else's toes. Also, it made way for constant business to be conducted with each other, a money chain that could circle forever. The pact also stated that no family could harm another or the people they had working under them. The peace lasted for a long time, but after Barry Tolliver, another family head, was killed, everything around them altered.

At first the war had been with Barry's son, Boogie, who unleashed his rage on everyone around him. And when he finally realized the error of his ways, it was too late. He'd already lit the spark that had led them all to their current space of feuding with the Chinese, the one that got Zo's father killed.

The Chinese family was relentlessly trying to seize the power of the five boroughs for themselves. Zo still felt a fire in his chest toward them and couldn't wait to get his hands on Tao Chen. He would pay for what he did to Marco. Zo dreamt many nights of what he would do once he got his hands on him. There would be days on end of torture drawn up specifically for him. But until then, Zo was just trying to keep everything afloat around him, and that meant hiding the warehouse slips showing that their last two weapons shipments at all locations had been short.

Zo snapped out of his trance and stepped backward out of the kitchen. Whoever had killed them must have still been in the house, but how had they gotten in, and past security undetected at that? It had never happened before as long as Zo had lived. His mind quickly went to finding his mother and Daniella. He turned around to run and find them, but he was stopped by a gun pointed dead in his face.

"Going somewhere?" a voice asked right before someone crept up behind him and knocked him out cold.

Copper. That was what the blood on Zo's tongue tasted like right before he spit it out. He had come to, but he barely had time to adjust to his surroundings before he was on the defense. His arms were tired as he tried to block the punches and kicks from three big men holding him captive. He could tell by their accents that they were Jamaican, but what he couldn't figure out was why they had broken in. They were relentless in their beatings, and at first his arms were on fire, but they quickly turned numb. He couldn't feel them to send them the strength needed to keep holding them up. His mother's prized white living room carpet was stained with his blood, and Zo knew seeing it would break her heart.

"Stop!" a voice boomed.

Instantly the blows ended, and the men moved back. Stepping from the kitchen was a husky Jamaican wearing a ruby red suit. He sported freshly twisted locs on the top of his head and a shaggy beard. The designer suit he wore didn't mask the obvious fact that he was rough around the edges. In his hand was a bottle of brandy, from which he took a big swig before tossing it to the ground, shattering it. Zo blinked the blood from his eyes and focused on the man as he got closer. He was taken aback when he saw that he recognized him. It was Jahmar Brown, a man who was born and raised in Queens. He'd moved and was supposedly a big thing in Boston now. Zo's family had been doing business with him for years. Why would he want to see Zo hurt?

"What the fuck do you think you're doing, Jahmar?" Zo panted, still trying to catch his breath. "You know who I am and what I can do to you!"

"I know who your father *was*." Jahmar's tone was low and menacing. He stepped closer to Zo and shook something in his hand like dice. "And I also know who he isn't anymore. He's dead."

"So you break into his family home to . . . what? Rob us of petty things?"

"I did see a few things that will be coming with me when I take my leave. But no, that's not why I'm here."

"Then tell me what you want."

"Before Marco's untimely end, I placed an order for a hundred thousand dollars' worth of weapons. Weapons that never came."

"If that's all this is about, I can get you your weapons. And I'll think about forgiving you for everything you've done so far."

To Zo it was a sensible offer. So much had already happened, and he just wanted them to leave. He didn't want anything to happen to his mama or his sister. He couldn't lose them, too, even if that meant letting the Jamaicans go untouched.

Jahmar looked at his men, and they all began laughing together. Jahmar stopped laughing abruptly and spat in Lorenzo's face. "That's what I think of your words."

"You're going to regret that," Zo said as saliva trickled down his face. Jahmar backhanded him so hard that his head snapped to the side. He forced the pain down and took a deep breath before glaring back into Jahmar's dark eyes. "You're going to regret that too."

"Am I supposed to fear a man who is at my mercy?" Jahmar scoffed. "I was supposed to jump for joy when the only thing offered to give me are the guns I paid for?"

"Isn't that what you're doing all of this for?"

"It was, until I saw a bigger picture being painted in front of me."

"And that is?"

"Queens. I want all of Queens."

"Here we go with this shit," Zo groaned. "You mother-fuckas and your thirst to control one of the five boroughs is starting to piss me off. Even with me dead, do you think my family will let some fucking Jamaican come and take my father's place?"

"How sure are you that they won't? I'm not blind or deaf," Jahmar told him. "I know all about the chaos that's been happening between the boroughs. The loyalty you all once had to each other is gone. The blacks killing the Asians, the Asians killing everybody. I've heard it all."

"What does that have to do with you?"

"Your families are falling apart. It's time for new blood to rule New York. So you will work under me. I will be the new weapons distributor. You will be the one who welcomes me into the fold and gets everyone else to fall in line."

"You want to know what I say to that?" Zo asked and sucked the blood from his teeth to spit at Jahmar's feet. "Fuck you. I would die before I piss on my father's memory like that."

Jahmar gave a tiny chuckle and kept shaking whatever he had in his hand. He stared at Zo for a few moments, taking in the defiant look on his face before looking down at his hand. Slowly he opened it and showed Zo what he was holding. Two hollow-tip bullets rested in his palm.

"These were the bullets I was going to use to end your life," Jahmar said evenly.

"You might as well get ready to use them, because I'm not doing what you want. I can't."

"I might have underestimated you, Lorenzo. Given the fact that you are Marco's son, I didn't think you'd be as nailed to the floor as him. Now *that* man could drive a tough bargain. But you I think I know how to break. You're going to give me what I want one way or the other."

Jahmar made a motion to one of the men standing close to Zo. He left the room, and Jahmar stared at Zo with an excited glint in his eye. Just as Zo was about to ask him what was tickling him, he saw something that made it feel like a hand was making a fist around his heart. Jahmar's henchman had returned to the room, but he wasn't alone. He had Zo's mother and sister in tow. His gun was pointed at the back of their heads as he forcefully pushed them onto the living room couch. Their eyes, mouths, and hands were bound, and they both had a few bloody gashes on their bodies.

"Mama! Daniella!" Zo shouted and tried to get to them, but Jahmar's fist slamming into his face stopped him.

He was knocked back, but that didn't stop him from trying again. He lunged for Jahmar when he found his footing, but the sound of guns cocking stopped him. He was helpless as he stared at his family sitting on the couch. They were going to die if he didn't do anything. Slowly, Jahmar put the two bullets he was holding into his magazine and placed it in his gun.

"I only have two bullets, so I'm thinking one close-up head shot will do it for the both of them. What do you think?" Jahmar said, standing in front of Christina and pointing the gun at her head.

"Don't!"

"Agree to my terms or your mother dies."

"I . . ." Zo's eyes fluttered to his mama, who sat up straight on the couch.

She showed no sign of fear although she heard Jahmar's threat. She had always been strong. She and Zo's papa had been the perfect match. She might have been being brave, but Zo had never been so afraid in his entire life. He would have rather died than to see her perish in front of him. He would give anything to save her life. Just as Zo opened his mouth to give Jahmar what he wanted, the sound of someone clearing her throat filled the room.

"That's enough, gentlemen."

The voice was soft but drenched with authority. Zo's eyes went to one of the living room entryways and fell on Diana, the head of the Dominican syndicate. Her frame seemed small standing in front of the army of men she'd brought with her, but her power spoke loudly. They wouldn't even breathe if she told them not to. Their guns were pointed at the four men holding Zo and his family captive, and the Jamaicans didn't dare make a move—except Jahmar.

"You wouldn't even get one shot off before this bitch's brain is splattered all over the wall behind her," he said, jabbing his gun toward Christina. "Put your weapons down!"

"All battles have casualties," Diana said with a bored expression. "Even if you kill her, you still die. You fucking idiot. Who taught you to negotiate?"

"Bitch, I—"

"I'm going to be short with you because I'm bored and I have business to discuss with Lorenzo," Diana said and eyed the Glock in his hands. "You see that little indicator there on the side of your gun? It's telling me that you don't even have a bullet in the chamber. Do you think you'll have time to cock your gun before . . . Actually, why am I still talking? Kill these sons of bitches."

The order was out of her mouth for only a millisecond before gunfire rang out. Jahmar was the first to get hit, and Zo couldn't say that he was sad to see his body twitch before dropping lifelessly to the floor. The others tried to shoot back, but it was no use. The Dominicans' bullets ate them alive. Once they were all dead, Diana went to untie the women on the couch. When she removed their face binds, Christina looked incredulously up at her.

"Casualties in war? You were going to let that mother-fucker shoot me!"

"He was never going to get that shot off," Diana assured her with a smirk.

"Yeah, yeah, yeah. You're late. I called you half an hour ago when I saw those motherfuckers pay off Eduardo and the rest of them."

"Eduardo?" Zo asked, wide-eyed. "Are you sure?"

"How else would they be able to get inside?" Christina shook her head with a disappointed expression on her face. "Sometimes even loyalty fades."

"Mama, why didn't you say anything?"

Zo couldn't hide his shock. Eduardo had been head of security for the estate for almost a decade. He had been responsible for keeping the Alverez family safe for so long that Zo couldn't believe he was capable of doing something so terrible. What would make him turn on his own?

"It all happened too fast. I barely had time to call Diana for help or get to Daniella in this big-ass house by the time they broke in. I'm just glad Diana showed up when she did. But Maria and Thomas . . ."

Christina's voice faded in sadness, and Daniella comforted her. Maria and Thomas had been more than just employees. They'd become her friends, too. However, Zo couldn't mourn them yet. His mind was on other things.

"Why would they betray us like this?" Zo asked, still puzzled by it all.

"I can tell you why," Daniella said, standing. "They think you're weak, Lorenzo. They don't believe you have what it takes to lead them the way *Papi* did. You have to show them. You have to find Eduardo and the rest of them and kill them."

"She is right, son," Christina agreed. "Your father was a strong man. He would not tolerate such insubordination, especially something that would put his family at risk. You will handle it?"

"I will, Mama."

"That brings me to what we need to discuss," Diana butted in. "Coincidentally, I was already going to head over here tonight, Caesar's orders. He fears that the Chinese may be planning another attack after their last failed attempt on his life. And after what happened at his event, we both agree that we're too old to be on the front lines. It's time."

"Time for what?" Zo asked.

"This is your war to fight. It's time for the next generation to take over completely."

Chapter 2

"It's all my fault. This is all my fault."

Boogie Tolliver never thought taking over his father's empire would create so much sadness in his life. He'd gone from the prince to the king of Brooklyn. He never wanted the crown, but it was on his head nevertheless. He held his face in the palms of his hands as he listened to the beeps of the machines connected to his girlfriend Roz's body. She'd been in a coma for days since she'd been shot. What was supposed to be an event celebrating New York's godfather, Caesar King, had ended in chaos and a lot of death. Boogie was hoping that the last casualty wouldn't be Roz. But with each moment that passed, she didn't seem to be making any progress. She'd lost so much blood, and even with the blood transfusion she'd received, her survival was still up in the air. He was coming to terms with the fact that no matter how much shouting at the doctors he did or how many prayers he sent up, it was out of his hands. Boogie hadn't seen or spoken to anyone since the day she was shot. He barely left her side. He'd felt regret before but never like that. If Roz died, he wanted to go right along with her.

"God, I know you can hear me. Don't take her from me, please. Bring her back. I'll do anything. Just bring her back to me. I don't have anything else."

"You have a lot of things. Including the mess you still need to clean up out there in the streets."

The voice came out of nowhere, but Boogie didn't need to look to know who it belonged to. He wiped his face and stood up with his back still turned toward the door.

"How did you find me, Caesar?"

"You were never lost. You've been here every day for the past week nonstop. Do you think you've been alone this whole time?"

"So you've been stalkin' me?"

"No, I've been protecting you. I've kept this entire hospital surrounded with men ever since Roz was admitted."

"I don't need your protection! Don't you know that all this street shit is the reason why I'm in this situation? I just want to go back to the way life used to be!"

"The blood that's running through your veins is why you're in this situation. And no, unfortunately we can't go back to the way life used to be. And admittedly, you had quite the hand in that. In fact, that's the reason you need all the protection you can get. Especially now."

There was something about the tone in Caesar's voice that made Boogie turn around. As usual, the elder man was sharp and dressed in a suit. The diamond cuff links shined under the bright overhead light. He looked to be back to himself after being badly wounded. He also had gotten his weight back up. There was a troubled expression on his face, and Boogie knew something had happened.

"What do you mean especially now?"

"It's Tao."

"He made another hit?"

"No. He's dead. His body was found hanging from a light pole in front of his own restaurant."

"Damn. Was it one of ours who did it?"

"My people know better than to act without an order. And I checked with the other boroughs, including yours. It was none of ours."

"Then who? Who would be bold enough to kill him and string him up in front of his own business?"

"I did some digging. And rumor has it that it was Ming. His son."

"What?" Boogie asked, surprised.

"Why do you look so shocked, especially after everything you've been through? The allure of power has made man do worse."

Caesar was right. One thing Boogie knew by then was that sometimes family would be the one to stab you in the back. He shook the thoughts of his mother from his mind. Trying to understand what she had done would always drive him to the brink of insanity. He would never understand.

"I guess the question that I really should be asking is why."

"I can only guess. And that guess is that he did it to send a message to the rest of them. To follow him or end up just like Tao."

"I thought they were big on loyalty and shit like that."

"They're loyal to the Triad, and now I have reason to believe that Ming has their full backing. . . ." His voice trailed off, and he looked away.

Boogie knew the look on Caesar's face. It was the look of a man who didn't want to deliver bad news. A part of Boogie didn't want to ask, but another part knew he would find out what it was one way or another.

"There's somethin' else, isn't there?"

"Roz's home. It was burned to the ground last night."

Boogie heard him but not with his ears. He heard Caesar with his body. He froze and sat on the words for a couple of seconds. The somber look in Caesar's eyes made Boogie almost afraid to ask.

"Bentley and Amber?"

"They weren't there. Bentley dropped the baby off to Morgan yesterday morning and then went to handle the affairs you've been neglecting."

Boogie ignored the slight dig and took the moment to be grateful. Roz wouldn't have forgiven him if something had happened to her brother or her child. However, his relief didn't take away the fact that someone was sending him a message.

"My men?" Boogie asked, speaking about the soldiers who patrolled his entire block.

"They unfortunately didn't make it. Your street is taped up. It wouldn't be wise to go back there."

"If you said the house is burned to the ground, there's no reason to anyway. I guess there's no need to ask if the Chinese were behind this."

"Even if we didn't already know, they made sure that we would. They left this behind on your sidewalk."

Caesar pulled out his phone and showed Boogie a picture. Drawn on his sidewalk was a circle, and in the middle was a Chinese symbol. When Boogie looked closer, he realized that the symbol had been drawn in blood.

"What does this mean?"

"It's the symbol of the Triad. I think they're warning us that this is just the beginning," Caesar told him, placing his phone back in his pocket. "I know you're going through something right now, son. But that doesn't mean the world outside of this hospital stopped. We're at war. A war—"

"That I created, I know. I remind myself about that enough. I don't need you to do it for me."

"If you know, then why aren't you out there fighting it? If you started it, you can end it."

"How?"

"That's something you and the others can figure out."

"Me and the others?" Boogie tried to make sense of the words.

"Diana and I have fought enough wars and lost enough friends. The time for us to rule has come and gone. It's time for the next in line to take your seats on the throne and put New York back together again. Hopefully you'll do a better job than us. Roz will be fine. I'll make sure of that. But you need to go, Boogie. The others will be waiting for you."

Caesar left the room, and Boogie stood there dumbfounded. He felt like a child who had just been told to figure it out on his own. He looked back at Roz and smiled sadly. She looked so peaceful, like she was having the nicest dream. Boogie went over to her and kissed her gently on the forehead.

"I have to go, baby. I have to clean up my mess. But I'll be back, I promise. You hear me? I love you."

Boogie inhaled a sharp breath, walking away from her and out of the room. He felt like he had taken so many losses that he needed a win. Caesar was right. It was time to get back in the game.

Once he was out of the hospital and inside his Lamborghini, he found himself just driving. He didn't have a specific destination in mind, but he trusted himself to get to where he was going. His thoughts were an ocean, and he was swimming freely in them. Before he knew it, he was at his destination. It was like he had blinked and had been teleported, but the truth was really just a case of highway hypnosis. He parked the car on the street and took a deep breath before looking out of the passenger window. He clenched his jaw tight as he stared at the burnt-up house. Although he told Caesar he wouldn't go there, he couldn't help himself.

The only thing still standing was the frame. Everything else was a heap of wood and ashes around it. He knew that he could just move Roz and Amber into the Tolliver family home, but he personally didn't even want to be there. There were just too many bad memories. And he didn't feel that the condo he owned was big enough for Amber to run around in. He would have to buy a new house, but that still wouldn't replace all of Roz's priceless items, and he knew that. It was the only time he was relieved that she wasn't conscious, because he didn't know how to look her in the face and tell her that once again things were screwed up because of him.

Boogie got out of the vehicle to get closer. He didn't know why, because even if he found anything he wanted to take with him, he couldn't. The smoke from the fire had made everything poisonous. He stepped over the hazard tape and began to move toward the rubble. However, before he could take another step, something else caught his eye. It was the sidewalk that Caesar showed him in the picture on his phone—the symbol of the Triad. It was something that would now be forever etched in his mind. They were letting him know that they were coming for him. There were only two possible endings, and both led to death.

"I didn't think you would be stupid enough to come here, but then again I knew you would."

The voice came from behind Boogie, but he knew who it belonged to before he turned. He'd heard it before, on that day at the big house. He turned around slowly, and sure enough there was Ming Chen standing in the middle of the street. Boogie glanced up and down for any sign of an entourage, but it seemed that Ming was alone. He returned Boogie's hard stare with a smirk.

"You must have known I was just thinkin' about how I'm gon' kill you. And everybody else close to you. You tried to murder my family."

"If I had tried to, they would be dead," Ming said evenly. "I waited until your friend and child were gone before I gave the order to burn this to the ground."

"I don't believe you."

"I wanted to show you how easy it is now for me to get through any of your security defenses. Your men are no match for mine. Even with Caesar thinking he was keeping you safe at the hospital, he wasn't. If I wanted you or anyone close to you dead, you would be dead."

"Then why am I still breathin'?"

"Are you as stupid as you look? I just said if I wanted you dead, you would be."

"So are you sayin' you don't want to kill me?"

"I do, but first I will make an offer."

"An offer? I guess I can humor you since we're here."

"I think we can come to an agreement to stop all the war and killing. You and the other families can continue to do business as you have been for all these years."

"But?"

"But you will have to pay me fifty percent of all your earnings every month."

"Bullshit. You're fuckin' crazy. I won't agree to that, and neither will they."

"Then you will all die."

"Not if I kill you first," Boogie said and reached for his gun.

Before he could untuck it, Ming made a slight gesture with his hand. Boogie froze when he saw his entire body lit up in red dots. Shock written all over his face, he looked at Ming, who was casually adjusting his shoulders in his suit jacket. Boogie's eyes went to the rooftops, trees, and bushes around him, but he couldn't spot a soul. He couldn't believe he'd been caught slipping with one of his own moves.

"Stealth is one of the greatest tricks of my people. Sit down with the others and tell them my offer. Don't look for me. I will find you," Ming said before turning and walking away.